P9-BJX-919

LET IT BE

BUTLER, VERMONT SERIES, BOOK 6

MARIE FORCE

DISCARDED

Let It Be
Butler, Vermont Series, Book 6
By: Marie Force

Published by HTJB, Inc.
Copyright 2020. HTJB, Inc.
Cover Design by Courtney Lopes
E-book Layout: E-book Formatting Fairies
ISBN: 978-1952793912

MARIE FORCE is a registered trademarks with the United States Patent &
Trademark Office.

If you're reading this book and did not purchase it, or it was not purchased
for your use only, then please return it and purchase your own copy. Thank
you for respecting the hard work of this author. To obtain permission to
excerpt portions of the text, please contact the author at
marie@marieforce.com.

Reading Order for Green Mountain/Butler, Vermont Series

The Green Mountain Series
Book 1: All You Need Is Love *(Will & Cameron)*
Book 2: I Want to Hold Your Hand *(Nolan & Hannah)*
Book 3: I Saw Her Standing There *(Colton & Lucy)*
Book 4: And I Love Her *(Hunter & Megan)*
Novella: You'll Be Mine *(Will & Cam's Wedding)*
Book 5: It's Only Love *(Gavin & Ella)*
Book 6: Ain't She Sweet *(Tyler & Charlotte)*

The Butler Vermont Series
Book 1: Every Little Thing *(Grayson & Emma)*
Book 2: Can't Buy Me Love *(Mary & Patrick)*
Book 3: Here Comes the Sun *(Wade & Mia)*
Book 4: Till There Was You *(Lucas & Dani)*
Book 5: All My Loving *(Landon & Amanda)*
Book 6: Let It Be *(Lincoln & Molly)*
Book 7: Come Together *(Noah & Brianna)*

CHAPTER ONE

*"Life is what happens to you while you're
busy making other plans."*
—John Lennon

Fridays were Lincoln Abbott's favorite day of the
workweek, and not just because they were the
only thing standing between him and two full days off to
spend with his wife, Molly. He also enjoyed Fridays because
his executive team—all of them his grown children—were
usually in good spirits as they prepared for the weekend.
Another thing to love about Fridays was that most weeks,
Linc enjoyed lunch at the diner with Molly and her dad,
Elmer, both of whom were at the top of Linc's list of favorite
people.

He loved everything about his life in Butler, Vermont,
from the breathtaking scenery to the entertaining town
moose named Fred to the Green Mountain Country Store,
Elmer's parents had founded the store, and Lincoln had
poured his heart and soul into for forty years, the last fifteen

of them as CEO. Mostly, though, he loved the family he and Molly had raised. Their ten children had grown into adults he loved, admired and was proud to consider friends and colleagues. Molly, their marriage and those ten kids were his greatest accomplishments.

As he crossed Elm Street on his way back to the office after lunch with Molly and Elmer, he took note of the work being done to rebuild the Admiral Butler Inn that had burned earlier in the year, nearly taking his son Lucas with it. Linc couldn't bear to think about that night or how close they'd come to losing their beloved Luc, who, like his identical twin brother, Landon, was a lieutenant in the Butler Volunteer Fire Department.

Linc shook off those morose thoughts and gave thanks once again for Luc's good health and his rapid recovery from injuries that might've killed a lesser man. Lucas had also saved the life of Amanda, who was now blissfully engaged to Landon.

His seven sons were in great shape from their many outdoor pursuits, including rock-climbing, skiing, snowboarding, mountain search and rescue and numerous other things that he and Molly were probably better off not knowing about. That conditioning had saved Lucas's life in the fire.

Linc's nephew Noah Coleman's construction company was rebuilding the inn, and Linc couldn't wait to see how it came together under Noah's leadership. Out of all the kids—ten Abbotts and eight Colemans—Noah was the enigma, the one who kept his distance from the family, especially since the dreadful breakup with his ex-wife, the details of which had been kept in lockdown. Linc kept hoping they'd get back the old Noah again. He'd once been a happy, outgoing kind of guy, but there'd been no sign of that Noah in years.

Linc had left Molly and her dad enjoying a cup of coffee and a slice of the apple pie their daughter-in-law Megan had made to return to the office for the weekly Friday afternoon staff meeting. They didn't really need the meeting, but Linc enjoyed getting everyone in the same room once a week to share ideas and energy. Some of their best initiatives had resulted from the meetings they tried to have weekly unless they had something better to do, such as a long weekend at their place in Burlington or their son Wade's wedding in Boston this past June.

Nothing came before family time, not even the business his father-in-law had entrusted him with after he retired. It was a huge honor for Linc to continue the legacy that Elmer's parents began and Elmer had continued, and to serve as the steward until one of his kids took the helm. He suspected it would probably be Hunter, but Linc was determined to let them figure that out for themselves. Any of the five who worked in the office with him would be qualified to take over when the time came, but that day was still a long way in the future. Linc was having way too much fun to think about retiring. As long as he and Molly could get away by themselves once in a while, they were happy with the status quo.

He loved the work of running an old-time country store and the challenge of maintaining the nostalgic feel of the place while applying modern business strategies to spark growth. Such as the catalog they'd launched in September that had doubled their monthly gross revenue in the three months it'd been in circulation, giving them their busiest holiday season in the company's history.

The catalog and the warehouse that fulfilled the orders had lit a spark of excitement within the company that was palpable, as had the intimate product line Linc had championed—to the dismay of his children—which had brought in scores of new customers. He often chafed against his children's more conservative approach to growing the business, but wasn't afraid to pull rank when it suited his purposes. That's exactly what he'd done with the intimate line, and he had no regrets there. Not to mention the product line had brought Amanda to town, and she and her daughter, Stella, would officially join their family when Amanda married Landon.

He went up the flight of stairs from the store to the executive offices where his nephew Grayson's fiancée, Emma, greeted him. Her sister, Lucy, was married to Linc's son Colton.

"How was lunch?" Emma asked.

"Excellent as always. Anything going on?"

"I put through a few calls to your voicemail, but nothing that sounded urgent."

"Thank you. I meant to ask earlier how Simone is doing with her new braces." Emma's daughter had gotten the braces the week before.

"She hates them, but we keep telling her she'll get used to them. She's not convinced yet."

"My kids hated them at first, too, but you're right. After a while, they forget about them."

"I hope so. She's pretty miserable."

"Poor baby."

The ringing phone took Emma back to work as Linc headed into his office to check his voicemail. At a quick glance, it seemed the others were still at lunch, but they'd be back in time for the meeting at one thirty. He listened to a message from Lucas's fiancée, Dani, who managed the warehouse for them.

"Hey, I wanted to let you know I'm not going to make the

meeting today. We're totally slammed here, and I need to stick around. I'll check in with you at Sunday dinner to find out what I missed. The good news is we're slammed. The bad news is we're slammed. Haha, see you."

Linc smiled at the message. She was right—it was great news they were slammed, but he'd have to talk to her about what they could do to support her and the warehouse team in the last days before Christmas. Dani was such a terrific addition to their team—and their family. She and Luc were great together, and seeing his son take on the role of father figure to Dani's one-year-old daughter, Savannah, had been nothing short of amazing.

His voicemail beeped with the next message.

"Lincoln. It's Charlotte. Your sister."

Shocked to the marrow of his bones by the sound of a voice he hadn't heard in forty years, he sat up straighter.

"I'm sorry to call you out of the blue, but we wanted you to know that Father is gravely ill and doesn't have much time left. He's asked to see you. He knows he has no right to ask, but he's asking anyway. If you would, please call me." With shaking hands, Linc grabbed a pen to write down the number she recited. "I'll understand if I don't hear from you, but I hope I do."

For a long time after the voicemail disconnected, Lincoln sat perfectly still, staring at a spot on the wall from a leak in the roof the previous winter. They'd gotten the roof fixed, but the wall still bore the watermark. And why was he thinking about a water stain on the wall when his sister had just dropped earthshattering news into his lap?

His father was dying and wanted to see him.

Lincoln had no idea what to do with this information. He hadn't heard a word from any member of his family since that dreadful day more than forty years ago when he'd been forced to make an unfathomable choice. He'd made that choice and had never regretted it, not for one second. But the heartache of what he'd lost had stayed with him, like a long-festering wound that refused to fully heal, despite a life of unimaginable joy.

For a second, he feared he might be sick as the tuna sandwich he'd eaten for lunch churned in his belly. He took a sip from a water bottle on his desk. Then he pressed the voicemail button on the phone and listened again to Charlotte's message.

The original Charlotte, his baby sister… Four of his children bore the names of his siblings, but none of them knew that. They never spoke of his family. By some sort of unwritten rule, the topic was left untouched by a group that dissected everything. It'd been a while since he or Molly had talked about that fateful summer in which so many things had been decided. With one phone call from his sister, he was right back there, being forced by his father to choose between the woman he loved more than anything and his original family.

He'd chosen Molly and had carried the pain of losing his mother and siblings with him every day since.

His mother had died years ago. He'd been told after the fact in a letter from his father's attorney that had come to the office weeks later. A few times over the years, he'd searched for his siblings online and on social media, but he'd found nothing about them, only news of the business itself. He had no idea who they'd married, if he had nieces or nephews, if they still worked for the family business or lived in the Philadelphia area, where they'd been raised.

He knew nothing about the people he'd been closest to as a child.

A quick glance at the clock told him he had fifteen minutes until the kids would be back for the staff meeting. If he was going to return Charlotte's call, he needed to do it now or be forced to wait until after the meeting.

Somehow he knew if he didn't make that call right now, he never would. He picked up the phone and dialed the number, holding his breath while he waited for her to pick up.

"Linc? Is that you?"

His phone number, bearing the distinctive 802 area code, must have shown up on her screen. "It's me."

"It's so good to hear your voice."

"You, too."

"I'm sorry to do this to you, but Father... He asked me to call you. He doesn't have much time left, Linc."

"What's wrong with him?"

"He's suffered from emphysema for years, and it's gotten progressively worse. The doctor told him this week to get his affairs in order. He said the only thing he needed to do was speak to you."

"I'm not sure what to say to that. It's been forty years..."

"I told him it was too much to ask of you, but he asked me to call anyway. No one would fault you if you chose not to come."

"I... I don't know." The thought of revisiting that pain was almost more than he could bear. "I need to think about it."

"I understand, but I recommend you think quickly. The doctor said he has a week, maybe two. He's in hospice care at home."

"I'll call you tomorrow."

"Linc... You have my number now. Even if you decide not to see Father, please call me when you have time to catch up. I... I've missed you so much."

Her softly spoken words brought tears to his eyes. His father's mandate had left a lot of carnage in its wake, and not just for him. "Likewise. Thanks for calling. I'll be in touch."

"I'll look forward to hearing from you."

Linc put down the phone and thought about what she'd said. His father wanted to see him. He didn't have much time left. His sister had missed him. Taken one at a time, any of these things would've been a bombshell. Taken together… It was more than he could process after decades of complete silence from his family. He'd made his choice, and he'd been forced to live with it, cut off from the people he'd loved first.

Molly. He needed her.

Just as he had that thought, his son Hunter came into the office. Tall and handsome, with dark hair and eyes, Hunter reminded Linc so much of the older brother his son had been named for, the brother he'd lost far too young.

"What's wrong?" Hunter asked, always perceptive.

"Nothing's wrong, but something came up, and I have to leave a little early. Would you run the meeting and check in later?"

"Of course. No problem."

Lincoln grabbed his coat and keys and headed for the door.

"Are you sure you're okay?"

"I'm sure, son." He squeezed Hunter's arm on the way by and stopped to speak to Emma. "I'll be home this afternoon if you need me."

Emma's brows knitted with concern. "Oh. Okay. Are you all right?"

"I'm fine, thank you. I'll see you Monday. Have a nice weekend."

"You, too."

He rushed down the stairs, eager to get out of there before he had to explain his abrupt—and unusual—early departure to the rest of his children. They knew him far too well and would see right through him the way Hunter and Emma had.

Linc got into his Range Rover and headed for home. He wasn't sure if Molly had other plans after lunch with her dad, but she'd end up at home eventually, and he'd be there, waiting for her to help him figure out what to do.

She always knew what to do, and he'd never needed her wisdom more than he did right then.

CHAPTER TWO

"Love is the flower you've got to let grow."
—John Lennon

*W*hen Lincoln got home, he realized he'd left George, one of his two yellow Labs, in town with his daughter Charley. She'd taken George with her on a lunchtime run and hadn't returned before Linc left. He'd have to retrieve George later, after he'd talked to Molly. He let out their other Lab, Ringo, and poured himself a glass of ice water.

He really wanted bourbon, but he needed to keep his head clear. Standing at the kitchen window, he gazed out at the snow-covered landscape that had become so familiar to him since he arrived in Vermont. Back then, he couldn't imagine hip-deep snow for months on end. Now it was as much a part of his life as his lovely wife, the barn they called home and the ten children they'd raised there.

Vermont ran through his blood, with her mountain peaks, aspens, evergreens, cool crisp air and pure, raw beauty. He'd been fortunate to travel widely, but he'd never been anywhere that had called to him the way this place had from the first time Molly brought him home with her.

He loved the way the house smelled of pine and spice this time of year, when Molly had their barn decorated for the holidays.

Ringo's excited barking a short time later alerted Lincoln to Molly's arrival.

She came in a minute later, chatting with the dog, who darted into the kitchen and then back into the mudroom, torn between wanting to be with both of them.

They'd wanted dogs, kids, a comfortable home and a life in Butler, Vermont. They'd gotten all those things—in spades.

Smiling, Molly walked into the kitchen, her cheeks red from the cold, her eyes sparkling the way they always did when she looked at him. "This is a nice surprise. Thought you had the staff meeting this afternoon."

"I did. I mean... I do. Hunter is handling it for me."

She took a closer look at him, insightful as always where he was concerned. "What's wrong, love?"

"Sit with me?"

"Did something happen? The kids..."

"Everyone is fine." He took her hand and led her to the kitchen table, the scene of so many of their most important conversations.

"You're scaring me," she said when they were seated next to each other.

"I'm sorry. My sister, Charlotte, called me."

Shock registered in her expression. "You... your... Oh. What did she want?"

"To tell me my father is dying and wants to see me."

She stared at him for a long moment, her eyes no longer sparkling. Now they were flat with the start of anger. "All this time... He wants to see you *now*? After he excommunicated you from his life, your mother's life, your siblings' lives?"

"Yes."

"I hope you told her to tell him where to go."

"Not exactly."

"Lincoln… You can't actually be thinking about *going* there. After everything he put you through…"

"I know."

"Are you?" she asked hesitantly. "Thinking about going there?'

"I don't know what to do. One part of me says screw him. Where's he been the last forty years? The other part…" He let out a deep sigh. "The other part is the dutiful son who still feels he needs to come when his father calls, even after all this time."

Molly stood and came over to him. "Make room."

He scooted his chair back so she could make herself at home on his lap.

She wrapped her arms around him and kissed his cheek. "How *dare* he do this to you!"

Lincoln had known she'd be angry, and with good reason. His father had been awful to both of them once upon a time, forcing him to make a dreadful choice. He leaned his fore-head against hers, drawing on her for strength the way he had for so long now. She and their family were the best things to ever happen to him. He had no doubt he was leading the life he was meant to, and nothing, not even a blast from the past, could change his mind about that.

"What'll you do?" Molly asked after a long silence.

"I suppose I'll have to go, or spend the rest of my life wondering if I did the right thing by not going."

Molly's deep sigh said it all. "I hate this for you. He has no right to tie you up in knots this way after decades of silence, especially four days before Christmas."

"No, he doesn't have the right, but that's never stopped him before."

"I'll never understand how you were raised by someone like that, but still turned out to be the kindest, most loving husband, father, uncle and grandfather."

"It's all thanks to my mother and a progression of kind-hearted nannies who taught me compassion and empathy. I certainly didn't get any of that from him."

"I want to say something," she said, "and it may not be the right thing, but it's how I really feel."

"You know you can say whatever you want to me, love, and I always want to hear it. Why do you think I came straight home to you after Charlotte called?"

"What I want to say is this—you don't owe him *anything*, Linc. Not one damned thing. We're taught to honor and respect our parents, but he's done nothing to earn your respect. He's ignored you for decades. He let your mother die without ever seeing or speaking to you again. He's never met your children or once inquired about your health or welfare in all that time. You owe him *nothing*, and you have every right not to reopen that old wound because he's suddenly grown a conscience in the final hours of his life."

Lincoln couldn't help but smile at her vehemence.

"What're you smiling about?"

"You. You're magnificent, and I love you more than anything."

"What's that got to do with your father?"

"It's got everything to do with him. Every time I see your gorgeous face or listen to your words of wisdom, you remind me of why I chose you, why I still choose you every day and twice on Tuesday."

"The fact that you ever had to choose is the problem. That never should've happened." She ran her fingers through his hair, straightening it while gazing into his eyes with care and concern and love. Always so much love. "What do you want to do? You know I'll support you no matter what, even if it means trekking to Philly four days before Christmas."

"I wouldn't ask you to go, love. I know how busy you are before the holidays."

"There's no way in hell you're going there alone, so let's not bother to have that fight."

Lincoln gathered her in close to him, weighing the pros and cons of the decision the way he would a business challenge. *Take the emotion out of it,* he always told the kids. Sometimes that was easier said than done.

The mudroom door opened, bringing a whoosh of cold air into the kitchen, which preceded George galloping in ahead of Hunter. "You forgot someone at the office."

"I realized that after I got home."

Hunter saw his mother sitting on his father's lap and paused inside the kitchen door. "Didn't mean to interrupt anything."

"You didn't," Linc said. "Come in, son. Your mother and I were just talking."

Hunter joined them at the table, taking the seat Molly had originally occupied. "Is everything okay? It's not like you to miss the Friday staff meeting."

As he gave George a scratch behind the ears, Lincoln hesitated. He wanted to tell his son what'd happened, but that would require him to share things he'd never discussed with any of his children.

"Tell him," Molly said softly. "It's time."

"You're kinda freaking me out," Hunter said, looking between them. "Someone had better tell me something."

Since there was no easy way to share this particular story, Lincoln went with the highlights—or rather, lowlights, such as they were. "You know I'm not in touch with my family."

Hunter nodded. "You've never said why, and we figured out a long time ago not to ask."

"I had a falling-out with my father."

"That's not exactly true," Molly said, glancing at Hunter. "Your grandfather gave your father a terrible ultimatum, and now he's on his deathbed and apparently having regrets. He asked your aunt Charlotte, who your father also hasn't heard from in forty years, to call and ask him to come."

"I have an aunt Charlotte?"

"And uncles Hunter, Will and Max. Hunter died at twenty after an accident."

Hunter absorbed the information in his usual contemplative way. "I'm sorry you lost him."

"It was the worst thing to ever happen to me, until my father forced me to choose between your mother and my family."

Hunter stared at him, incredulous. "He forced you to choose…"

"Yes, and when I chose your mother, I never heard from any of them again, except a single letter from my father's attorney letting me know my mother passed away several years ago."

"God, Dad. I'm so sorry. That's unbelievable."

"It was a long time ago," Linc said with a sigh.

"And it was just as unbelievable then as it is now," Molly added.

"What are you going to do?" Hunter asked.

"I haven't decided yet."

"We need a family meeting," Hunter said. "Isn't that how we always make the big decisions?"

"Yes, but…" Lincoln hesitated at the idea of sharing the ugly story with the whole family.

"Let us help you the way you've always helped us, Dad."

"I think it's a good idea," Molly said. "And Hunter's right. It's what we do when there're decisions to be made."

Though he hesitated to burden his children with his concerns, Lincoln had to acknowledge they were right about how the family addressed big decisions, and now that the proverbial cat was out of the bag, there was no putting it back in. "Okay."

"I'll call the others," Hunter said, rising to use the phone.

"It's the right thing to tell them," Molly said when they were alone.

"Are you sure about that?" Linc asked with a small smile.

"They're the wisest people I know, other than you and my father. They'll know what to do."

"You should have Elmer come, too. It's not a family meeting without him."

"Hunter," Molly said. "Call Gramps, too."

"Will do."

Molly stood. "I suppose I ought to see about some food for this meeting."

"Hey, Mol?"

"Yes?"

"Thanks, you know, for having my back."

"Always have, always will. No matter what you decide to do, you have us. We won't let anyone, even your own father, hurt you." She kissed his forehead and then went to see about food for the troops. There was never a time when their children couldn't eat, but the thought of food with this decision weighing on him turned Linc's stomach.

His thoughts were all over the place, but he kept coming back to the moment that changed his life in ways he couldn't have imagined, the first time he'd laid eyes on young Molly Stillman, fresh off a thirty-hour bus ride from Vermont to Mississippi to spend a summer building homes for those who'd lost theirs in a devastating hurricane the year before.

She'd been a recent graduate of Middlebury College, wanting to see more of the country and volunteer to help others before she went to work for the family business in Vermont. Back then, she'd had long honey-colored hair, freckles on her nose and an inquisitive nature that had immediately intrigued him. He saw young Molly in all three of their daughters—in Hannah's curiosity, in Ella's kindness, in Charley's determination.

Fresh out of grad school at Yale, Linc was volunteering on the housing project before spending a post-graduate year at Oxford. As a lifelong Anglophile, he'd dreamed of living in the UK and retracing the steps of The Beatles, his favorite band of all time. The two months in Mississippi were supposed to have been a brief interlude before he got on with the rest of his life.

Little had he known then that those two months would change everything.

～

THE FIRST THING LINC HAD NOTICED WHEN HE ARRIVED IN Gulfport, Mississippi (population 39,600 at the time), was the heat. He'd been told it would be hot, but nothing could've properly prepared him for the thick blanket of humidity that made it almost hurt to breathe. Thankfully, Gulfport benefited from the sea breezes off the Gulf of Mexico, which provided a bit of relief.

He'd been met at the bus depot by Joseph Tolman, a tall, muscular Black man with a big smile and a crushing handshake. "Thanks so much for coming." He gestured for Linc to follow him to his pickup truck. "We need all the help we can get to finish this project in time to receive the second half of our federal funding."

In the wake of Hurricane Frederic the year before,

Tolman and several local contractors had committed to building a hundred and fifty affordable housing units by September 1 and had advertised nationally for volunteers willing to spend a summer learning on the job. Linc had been immediately intrigued by the opportunity to acquire practical skills while also helping people before he left for Oxford.

Since they'd lost his older brother Hunter three years earlier, nothing had been the same. Linc had grappled with his own grief after the staggering loss and had found it harder to be home, where pervasive sadness hung over their family. Spending the summer in Philadelphia hadn't been an option he'd been willing to entertain. When he'd heard about the project in Mississippi, he'd jumped at the chance to have something else to do.

"My friend who told me about your project said it wouldn't matter that I don't have any construction experience," Linc said.

When Joseph started the engine, AC/DC's new song, "You Shook Me All Night Long," came blasting out of the radio. Smiling, Joseph turned down the volume. "Your friend was right. We'll teach you what you need to know and rough up those soft hands in the process."

Linc laughed at the teasing jab that was delivered in the sweetest Southern accent. "I've been in school my entire life, or at least that's how it seems."

"Now it's time for some life skills."

"That's the idea."

"We work six days a week from sunup to sundown, but Sundays are all yours. We have almost seven miles of white sand beaches here in Gulfport."

"I read about that and can't wait to check it out. I can see myself spending a lot of Sundays there." Some of his favorite summers as a kid had been spent at the Jersey Shore with his grandparents, who'd had a summer home there.

"We've set up a campsite for the volunteers. It's nothing fancy, but it has everything you need."

"I'm sure it's great."

"When we realized we were in danger of missing our deadline to keep our federal funding, one of my partners suggested we put out a call for volunteers to the colleges. We really appreciate y'all coming."

"I appreciate you keeping me from having to spend the summer at home under my father's thumb."

"It's a pretty strong thumb, is it?"

"You have no idea. He's waiting for me to finish school and come into the family business."

"Which is?"

"Commercial real estate."

"Sounds exciting."

Linc laughed. "Not so much, but it pays the bills." The company was enormously successful, thanks to his father's vision and hard work. However, as the date got closer for Linc to join the company's executive team, he felt more and more trapped in a life of someone else's design.

"And that's what you want to do?" Joseph asked.

"I'm not exactly excited about it, if that's what you're asking, but that's the plan." All their plans had changed when Hunter died, and his father turned his sights on Linc as the new heir apparent. What Linc wanted didn't seem to matter, but since he didn't have a viable alternative, he'd gone along with his father's plan for him, albeit reluctantly.

"Huh," Joseph said.

"It's okay to say what you really think."

"Then I'll just say life is short. You should do what makes you happy, not what's expected of you."

"I couldn't agree more, but I've yet to find anything that makes more sense to me than the family business."

"Maybe you haven't been looking in the right places."

"I suspect that might be the case, which is why I jumped at the chance to spend the summer somewhere I've never been, working on something meaningful."

"The work you'll do here will mean so much to so many. We have a hundred and fifty families who were displaced by the storm lined up to get the first group of new houses. Many of them will be first-time homeowners, and they're so excited."

"It's a wonderful thing you're doing."

"I think so, too, but it's turned out to be far more stressful than we expected due to the rigid deadlines that come with federal funding. It's giving me gray hair."

Linc figured Joseph to be in his late thirties, and sure enough, he had a few grays in his otherwise dark hair. "It'll be worth it in the end when those families are happily settled."

"Keep telling me that." Joseph hooked a left onto a dirt road that led to the campsite where a bunch of tents had been set up. "Y'all have your own tents, but you'll share the bathrooms," he said, pointing to a building to the far left.

In another large tent with open sides, a group of people bustled about.

"Food," Joseph said when he saw Linc looking at the larger tent. "My wife, Keisha, and several of the other wives are in charge of feeding the volunteers. Keisha also runs the business side of things for my company, while taking care of our kids."

"You all are busy."

"You have no idea. Come meet my bride and the others."

Lincoln got out of the truck and followed Joseph into the tent. "This is Lincoln Abbott from Pennsylvania by way of

Yale. Linc, this is my wife, Keisha, our daughter, Jasmine, my business partner, Desmond, his wife, Charity, and their daughter, Shanda."

Linc shook hands with the adults and bent to say hello to little Shanda, who was about three. "Nice to meet you all."

"You, too." Keisha had a warm, welcoming smile, golden-brown skin and bright brown eyes. Her braided hair was captured in a high ponytail to keep it out of her way while she worked. "You have no idea what you've signed on for around here."

"That's probably true, but something smells really good."

"We're going to work you hard, but one thing I can promise is that you'll eat like a king," Joseph said.

Linc's mouth watered from the aromas coming from the pans. "Sounds like a fair deal to me."

CHAPTER THREE

"A dream you dream alone is only a dream.
A dream you dream together is reality."
—John Lennon

inc smiled as he remembered his arrival in Mississippi and the warm welcome he'd received from Joseph and Keisha, who were his and Molly's good friends to this day. They'd made a lot of good friends that summer, people they'd stayed close to in the ensuing years. That summer had been all about heat, hard work, good food, great friends, life lessons and love.

Speaking of love, Molly came back to the kitchen with their grandson, Caden, in her arms. The little guy chirped with excitement at the sight of Linc, who reached for him.

Molly handed him over.

Linc snuggled the sweet-smelling baby and kissed the top of his head. "Where's your daddy, pal?"

"In the shower," Molly answered. "He said he'll be down in a few minutes for the family meeting."

Max had come home from work at midday to take Caden to an appointment, and so Molly could go into town for her weekly lunch with Linc and Elmer. Under normal circumstances, Max would be on his way back to work—either at the mountain with Colton or the tree farm with Landon.

But since Linc had received that bombshell phone call, nothing about this day was normal for any of them.

"Are you okay, Dad?" Hunter asked.

Linc glanced at his son. "I'm okay. Of course it's upsetting, but it's nothing to worry about."

"That's good," Hunter said, visibly relieved.

It was astonishing, really, how much it still hurt, even after all this time. As he held his grandson close, he tried to tell himself that the family he'd created with Molly had more than filled the void of the one he'd lost. But it hadn't. Not completely. How could you ever "replace" the people you'd grown up with? He simply couldn't imagine any of his children being estranged from him and Molly or one another.

When the kids were younger and squabbling the way siblings did, Linc was forever reminding them that the best friends they'd ever have in their lives were the people right in their home. His children had heard that often enough that they'd taken it to heart and remained "thick as thieves," as Elmer liked to say, as adults.

Lincoln counted that as one of the greatest achievements of his life, because he knew all too well that it didn't always work out that way, that the bonds of family could be far more fragile than they appeared.

Over the next half hour, the kids trickled into the barn. First Ella, then Landon, Colton and Will. Hannah came with baby Callie, and Lucas showed up still wearing his fire department uniform. He'd been so thankful to return to work after being sidelined for almost two months following the fire at the inn. It was a relief to see him healthy, strong and in uniform.

Max came downstairs, fresh from the shower and immediately took note of Caden snuggled up with his dad. He was such a great dad to his little boy.

"What's on the docket?" Charley asked, her cheeks red from the cold.

"I'll tell you when Wade gets here."

"I'm here," Wade said, coming in with Elmer right behind him.

"That's all of us, Dad," Hunter said, always the leader of the pack.

"Let's go in the family room," Linc said, taking note of the unusual apprehension in his children's expressions and posture.

He followed them into the large but cozy room they'd decorated with multiple sofas when everyone still lived at home. They'd spent a lot of time there together, watching movies and sports and playing games.

Caden snuggled into Linc's embrace as if the little guy knew he needed some extra love just then.

Molly sat next to him, her hand on his leg. As she had from the very beginning of their journey, she was worth every sacrifice he'd made to be with her.

"Thanks for coming, everyone."

"You're kinda freaking us out, Dad," Charley said in her typically blunt style.

"Sorry to worry you." After a deep breath, he took the plunge. "You know I never talk about my family. My original family, I should say. I'm sure you've wondered why we don't see them or hear from them. It's not something I like to think about, let alone talk about, which is why I've steered clear of the subject. My father… He's a difficult, exacting man who likes to be in control of everything in his world, especially his children. When my older brother, Hunter, was killed in an accident when he was twenty, we were shattered."

"God, Dad," Hannah said. "I'm so sorry you lost him."

"It was brutal, and my father… He became more unyielding than ever after we lost Hunter. As his eldest living son, it was understood, by him, that I'd take Hunter's place, come into the family business like my brother was supposed to and take over for him when he was ready to retire."

"What was the family business?" Will asked.

"Commercial real estate in Philadelphia."

"What happened to your brother?" Wade said.

"He was hit in the head with a boom while sailing and was knocked overboard. The autopsy determined that he drowned."

"I'm so sorry, Dad," Ella said.

"It was an awful, shocking loss, especially since Hunt was such a skilled sailor." Linc thought of his late brother and his other three siblings just about every day. He retrieved worn family photos from his wallet and handed the first one to Hunter. "That's the uncle you were named for."

Hunter studied the image. "I look like him."

"Yes, you do. Here's one of all of us." He gave the second photo to Hannah. "My sister, Charlotte, and my other brothers, Will and Max, are in that one."

"You named us after them," Max said.

"We did, because I never stopped missing them." The raw pain of their initial split had been replaced, over time, by a feeling of nostalgia for the years they'd spent together. Back then, he'd been naïve to think that nothing could ever come between them. He'd found out otherwise in the most painful way possible.

"Since I didn't really have a better plan for myself, I went along with my father's plan for me after Hunter died. I wanted to keep the peace and not upset anyone after what we'd already been through." Linc forced himself to continue the story, determined to get it over with once and for all. "I mean, it's not like he was trying to hand over a crappy business. Quite the contrary. It was a thirty-million-dollar-a-year enterprise at that time, and from what I've seen and heard, it's only grown in the ensuing years."

Hunter let out a low whistle.

"In the back of my mind, always, was this niggling feeling that I wasn't meant for the commercial real estate business. But as long as I did what was expected of me, I was in my father's good graces. I had one more year of school planned at Oxford, which I'd insisted on out of fear that I might never get to the UK if I didn't make that happen, and then it would be time to go to work. I was resigned, if not very excited about it."

He glanced at Molly and smiled. "And then I met your mother."

AT THE END OF HIS FIRST FULL DAY WORKING ON THE construction site, Lincoln was tired, dirty, sweaty and sore. He'd had a true comeuppance when it came to realizing how easy college and grad school had been compared to the work he was doing now.

"How you holding up, Yank?" Joseph asked with a good-natured grin.

"I'm wrecked."

Joseph threw his head back and laughed. "You'll get used to it. Eventually."

"I'll have to take your word for that." Lincoln stretched the kinks out of his back that'd come from hauling building supplies from the delivery point to houses in various stages of construction. They were located around a wide swath of green space that would be used as a community gathering place once the development was completed.

Some of the houses were only framed, while others were much closer to completion. Joseph had told him that different teams worked on different houses, from framers to drywallers to finish carpenters, with plumbers and electricians coming and going as needed.

Lincoln could only imagine the coordination that went into the dizzying activity.

"Hey, Joseph," one of the foremen called from a house a few hundred yards from where they were standing. "We've got a problem you need to see."

"Ugh, it's always something." Joseph checked his watch. "Our last volunteer is arriving at five thirty. Would you mind taking my truck to pick her up at the bus station?"

Linc desperately wanted a shower, a change of clothes and something to eat, but he took the keys from Joseph, who had far more to contend with than Linc ever had.
"Happy to."

"Thanks a million. Bring her back here, and I'll drop you both at the campground on the way home."

"Will do."

"Do you remember how to get there?"

"I think so."

Joseph gave him verbal directions that Linc tried to commit to memory, hoping he wouldn't get lost. "You're looking for Molly Stillman."

"I'll find her."

As Lincoln drove into town, he took in the sights along the way. Families were gathered on spacious front porches, kids played in parks, and teenagers huddled together in groups. He passed an antique store, a diner, the post office, an art gallery and a variety of other shops and restaurants. Having never lived in a small town, he was fascinated by the slower pace, the sense of community and the obvious close-ness of the town's residents.

The farther he got from town, the more houses became dilapidated, overgrown, neglected. Some bore obvious damage from the hurricane. He felt good knowing he would help to make a difference for the families who'd benefit from their project, but the need was obviously much greater than a hundred and fifty houses.

Absorbed in the observations, he nearly missed the last turn for the bus station and realized he needed to turn only when he saw a bus pulling out of the road that led to the station. He parked and got out of the truck. Now that he'd arrived, he wondered how he'd recognize someone he'd never met.

And then he spotted a woman standing alone, a backpack at her feet, and walked over to her. "Are you Molly?"

She looked up at him, and *whoa*. Pretty. That was the first word that popped into his mind. When she smiled, his entire system went haywire as he took in her gorgeous face. She had long honey-colored hair, golden brown eyes and a sprin-kling of freckles across her nose that he found ridiculously adorable.

"Are you Joseph?" she asked.

It took him a full ten seconds to realize she expected him to reply. He blinked, cleared his throat and shook his head. "I'm Lincoln Abbott, one of the other volunteers. Joseph sent me to pick you up."

"I'm Molly Stillman."

He shook her outstretched hand, wondering how an average handshake could feel so far above average. "Nice to meet you. I came right from working all day at the site, so sorry to be picking you up filthy."

"No worries."

Linc bent to pick up her bag and saw that she had a second one slung over her back. "Is this everything?"

"Yep. I was told to travel light, and holy crap, it's hot."

"This is nothing." Linc led the way to Joseph's truck. "Wait until you see what midday is like."

"Can't wait," she said with a wry grin that he caught out of the corner of his eye. "Have you been here long?"

"Just since yesterday."

"Where're you from?"

"Philadelphia originally, but I've spent the last six years in New Haven, Connecticut."

"What's in New Haven?"

"Yale."

"Ah. I see."

He held the passenger door to the truck for her. "What about you? Where're you from?"

"A tiny little town in Vermont called Butler. I just graduated from Middlebury and jumped at the chance to get out of Vermont and experience something new before I start work in the fall."

"What're you doing for work?"

"Joining the family business," she said with a decided lack of enthusiasm that he could certainly relate to.

"What's the business?"

"A country store that my grandparents founded."

"That sounds fun."

"Does it? To me, it sounds… small." She winced and quickly added, "But it's fun, too."

Lincoln thought about what she'd said and tried to contend with his unprecedented reaction to her as he rounded the front of the truck and got in the driver's side. He'd had his share of girlfriends, but he'd never met anyone as lovely as Molly Stillman from Butler, Vermont.

"What's the store like?"

"It's an old-time country store, full of nostalgia and products you used to be able to get that are now hard to find. Plus housewares, toys, health stuff and, of course, maple syrup and cheese, two things Vermont is famous for."

"It sounds amazing."

"It is. Don't get me wrong. It's a very special place, and I've loved it all my life. One of my earliest memories was going to work with my dad on Saturdays and getting to pick out penny candy to bring home to my little sister."

"That's a sweet memory."

"Ha, no pun intended, right? All my memories of the store are sweet, and I really do love it. It's just that I'm not sure I want to spend my whole life working there, you know?"

He knew all too well. "I get it. I'm expected to join my family's business, too."

"What's your business?"

"Commercial real estate."

"That sounds more interesting than a country store."

"You might be surprised to hear I have zero interest in it. I'm giving myself this summer and next year in England to work up some enthusiasm."

"What's in England?"

"Oxford. I'm doing a postgraduate year there, which is a dream come true. I have a little thing for the Beatles, and it's been a longtime goal to spend a year in England."

"A little thing for the Beatles," she said, laughing. "I have a feeling you might be understating it if you're going to spend a year in England because of your love of a band."

"I might be understating it a tiny bit."

"Tell me the truth. You're obsessed, right?"

"What's the next level above obsessed?"

"Sociopathic?"

"That might be about right."

Her laughter sent a strange shiver of sensation darting

through him, filling him with an acute awareness of another human being that was all new to him.

"Which Beatle is your favorite?"

"Like… you want me to *choose* one of them?" He glanced over at her to see her smile.

"Yes. Just one."

"Oh God, how do I choose?"

"Come on. Surely someone has asked you this before."

"They have, and I've always refused to pick one, but something tells me you aren't going to let me off the hook that easily."

"You'd be right about that. Man up and choose."

Linc groaned loudly and dramatically. "Do you promise never to tell the others I picked one of them?"

"I solemnly swear."

"John," he said through gritted teeth.

Cupping her ear, she said, "What was that? I didn't quite hear you."

"John! Are you happy now?"

"Not until you tell me why you chose him."

"You're killing me here, but I chose him because he's not just an amazing musician. He's also a poet. His lyrics are just… They're life."

"What's your favorite Beatles song?"

"I can only have one?"

"In this instance, yes."

"Are you sure you didn't just graduate from law school? I feel like you might've missed your calling as a prosecutor."

Again, her laughter touched and delighted him.

"If you're going to force me to choose, then I'd say, 'Let It Be,' even though Paul wrote that one and John allegedly hated the song."

"You're going to think I'm lying, but that's my favorite, too. Although, I'm not all that into the Beatles."

"Wait. What did you just say? You're not that into the Beatles?"

"You heard me right. I'm more of a Rolling Stones kinda girl."

"At least they're still British."

"You really have a thing for the Brits, huh?"

"I've always been fascinated by the monarchy and British history, which was my double major in college along with business, so I guess it stands to reason I'm into British music, too."

"Who else besides the Beatles?"

"I love Queen, the Stones and the Who. I'm digging the Clash lately, but the Beatles will always be my number one."

"What do you think of Wings?"

"I like them, but not like I love the Beatles."

"I'm sensing a pattern here."

"You've already decided I'm a sociopath." He couldn't recall the last time he enjoyed a conversation so much.

"That's true."

"Tell me more about Vermont. I've never been there."

"It's the prettiest place you'll ever see. Mountains and trees and beautiful lakes. And when it snows, it's magical. Sometimes, the snow is hip-deep, and even then, I still love it. A lot of people hate the snow, but not me. I don't think I could live somewhere that doesn't get snow, but then again, I've never wanted to live anywhere but Vermont."

He could hear in every word she said how much she loved her home state.

She watched the world go by outside the passenger window as they drove through the area he'd seen before, made up of houses in need of repairs. "It's a little overwhelming to see up close."

"It is. It makes you realize how important the construction project is to so many people."

"We're going to leave here wishing we could've done more."

He already liked her more than just about any woman he'd ever met, but after she said that, he suspected he could love her.

～

"WE MADE SOME INCREDIBLE MEMORIES THAT SUMMER." Molly picked up the story, smiling at him the way she had since the first day they met. He never had gotten over the way her smile lit up her entire face. Making her smile had been one of his favorite things since their beginning.

"Don't say anything that can't be unheard," Lucas said warily.

"Haha, we'll spare you the gory details," Molly said. "Your dad and I were immediately best friends. We ate together, worked together, hung out after work, went to the movies."

"She took me to see *The Shining* and *Friday the 13th*," Linc said, shuddering. "I wanted to see *Airplane!* That's when I found out your mother is diabolical."

"We knew that," Will said. "Remember when she picked *The Shining* for family movie night, and we didn't sleep for three days?"

Molly laughed. "That might've been a parenting mistake."

"Do you *think*?" Charley asked.

"What can I say? I've always loved the scary stuff. I can't help it if you're all like your father—a bunch of babies."

"Don't lump me in with them," Wade said.

"Except for you, Wade. You're the only one who'd watch scary movies with me."

"Mama's boy," Landon said on a cough.

Wade flipped him the middle finger.

"Anyway," Linc said, amused by his children as usual, "as

the summer went on, your mom and I began to realize we had serious feelings for each other, and the reality of being separated after the summer was starting to loom large. We had our first real fight over what we were going to do when the summer ended."

"And it was a doozy," Molly added.

CHAPTER FOUR

"Love is all you need."
—Paul McCartney

The days in Mississippi took on a predictable rhythm—breakfast with the group of volunteers who'd become like family to him and Molly, followed by a long day of hard work in the broiling sun. Molly, who claimed she never tanned, had watched her skin turn a golden brown over the course of the summer.

On Sundays, the one day they had off, they left camp first thing in the morning to go to the beach for the day before dinner at Joseph's mother's home, which had become the highlight of their week. Miss Anthea, as she'd told them to call her, could cook like no one Linc had ever met, and the thought of her Sunday dinners had him drooling all week.

She'd also taught them an appreciation for the blues, bringing in an array of local musicians to play each week, hoping to send their volunteers back to their homes with a newfound love for the music Mississippi had made famous.

"Wonder what Miss Anthea is making today," Linc said.

"Is it okay to hope it's chicken? I've never in my life had chicken as good as hers."

"Or pulled pork or beans and rice or jambalaya or anything she makes."

"And the *cornbread*…" Molly moaned from her spot on the blanket next to him. "The cornbread is *to die for.*"

"It really is. And now I'm starving."

"Want to get a hot dog?" she asked.

"I do, in a minute. But first I want to talk to you."

"About what?"

"About this, us…"

"Oh."

For a second, Linc worried he might've read things wrong, but he hadn't. He was one hundred percent sure she felt the same way about him as he did about her. As July slipped into August, he was becoming increasingly more concerned about how he'd live without her in his daily life when they went their separate ways in three short weeks.

"What do you want to talk about?"

"What happens after this summer."

"You're going to Oxford, and I'm going home to Vermont. That's what's happening."

"What if…"

She put her hand on top of his, her touch sending a bolt of sensation through him the way it always did. "Don't, Linc," she said softly. "Don't go there."

"Why not?"

"Because. We both know what this is—and what it isn't."

"All I know is that in the course of seven weeks, you've become the most important person in my life, Mol. I want to be where you are."

"You're going to England."

"I don't know," he said, giving voice to his reservations for the first time. "I may have something else in mind now."

She surprised him when she got up from the blanket and walked away.

His eyes were drawn to the spectacular sight of Molly Stillman in a bikini. Front or back, the view was outstanding. He followed her to the water's edge, where she stood gazing out at the Gulf of Mexico. In the distance, he could make out the hulking towers of the oil rigs that populated the gulf.

"Talk to me, Molly. Don't run away."

Linc couldn't believe it when he saw tears in the eyes of the most fearless, free-spirited woman he'd ever met. He couldn't bear to think he'd made her cry, so he put his arm around her and drew her into his embrace. "Tell me."

"You're going to England. We're not going to even talk about anything other than that."

"Why not?"

"Because! It's your dream. It's what you've wanted your whole life, and you're *this* close to getting it. There's no way in hell I'm going to be the reason you don't go to England."

"What if my dream has changed?"

She pulled back from him, shaking her head. "A dream you've had all your life doesn't change in seven weeks."

"Says who?"

"Says me."

"England isn't going anywhere," he said.

"I'm not going to discuss this further. You have a plan for your life, and it's one you were happy with."

"Until I met you and discovered a whole new possibility."

She crossed her arms, her pose and expression defiant. "And what's that?"

"You and me, maybe a couple of kids, as many dogs as we can handle, a house in the country and decades together."

"You... That... Stop it right now, Lincoln Abbott."

She took off, and again he followed, taking her by the arm to stop her from getting away. All of a sudden, it had become essential to him that she not get away. "What if I tell Oxford I'm not coming this year?"

"That's not happening. I refuse to be the reason you give up your dream."

He tipped her chin up and kissed her. "I love you."

"*What? You do not love me!* We've had fun. That's all this is. *Fun.*"

"That's how it started out, but it's way more than that for me now. I love you, and I'm going to keep telling you that until you believe me. I want to be wherever you are, even if that means living in a small town in Vermont."

"I'm not listening to this anymore." Molly stormed off toward the blanket, grabbed her coverup, towel and bag and headed for where they'd parked the bikes they'd borrowed from Joseph and Keisha. She'd already taken off toward camp by the time Lincoln jumped on the other bike to follow her.

Back at camp, which was deserted on the one day the volunteers took for themselves, she went directly to her tent and zipped it closed, even though it was broiling and would be unbearable with the tent sealed off.

He decided to give her some space, to take a shower and figure out his next move.

MOLLY SAT INSIDE THE ROASTING COCOON OF HER TENT AND tried to get herself together. How could he *love* her? He barely knew her.

Except that wasn't exactly true. She'd told him things about herself that no one else knew, such as how much she wanted to be a mother and how little interest she had in her family's business. In this day and age, a woman was supposed to want a career of her own, but all she wanted was a family. And her sister, Hannah, felt the same way, leaving both of them in a bad spot as the youngest children of Elmer and Sarah Stillman, proprietors of the Green Mountain Country Store. Their older siblings already had lives and homes of their own elsewhere, so it had fallen to her and Hannah to inherit the business.

Molly and her sister had frequently talked about what they were going to do after college when they'd face a come-to-Jesus moment on the business their grandparents had started decades ago.

They didn't want it.

Their father couldn't wait to bring his girls into the business.

Her plan was to give the business a few years so she could say she tried before she hopefully got married and had a family. The one thing she knew for certain is that she'd never disappoint her beloved father by not showing up to work at the store when she got home. Regardless of what she wanted or didn't want, she loved him too much to let him down.

A man with dreams of spending a year in England followed by his own family obligations didn't fit into her plans. Even if she liked him more than she'd ever liked anyone since she lost her beloved Andrew while still in high school.

Okay, so maybe she loved Linc a little bit, too.

Or maybe she loved him a lot and couldn't imagine life without him after working and living side by side for weeks. And that made her feel guilty because she'd promised herself she'd never love anyone the way she'd loved Andrew.

How could this be happening?

Resting her head on her knees, she felt confused and thrilled and terrified all at the same time. Lincoln Abbott, the nicest, handsomest, sexiest, smartest man she'd met in all the years since she lost Andrew, *loved* her. So why was she hiding out in her tent when Lincoln Abbott loved her? Because she didn't want him to change his plans for her. He would hate her for that someday, and that would kill her.

But maybe when he came back...

She unzipped the tent and spotted him returning from the shower, wearing only a pair of shorts. The summer of hard work had left him with a chiseled, muscular body that had her imagining things she couldn't afford to think about when she was trying to talk him out of loving her.

He caught her staring at him and smiled as he walked over to her tent. "I wondered how long you were going to broil in there."

"I... I'm sorry I behaved that way."

"No apology necessary."

"Yes, it is necessary. You said something lovely to me, and I acted like a... I don't know what, but it wasn't an appropriate response."

"It's fine. I still love you."

"Lincoln."

"Molly."

His lips quivered with amusement while his blue eyes lit up with delight at the sight of her, the way they had from the start.

"Will you come in for a minute?"

"If I must."

And he was funny, always making her laugh over the silliest things. Molly scooted over to make room for him in her tiny tent. When he was settled next to her, she summoned all the courage she possessed to look him in the eye. "I probably love you, too."

He raised a brow. "Only probably?"

She swallowed the huge lump in her throat and tried to ignore the sweat running down her back. "Definitely."

"That's the best news I've ever heard."

"Better than getting accepted to Oxford?"

"A million times better."

"Here's what I think we ought to do… We should take this year while you're in England to make sure this is what we really want. We can write to each other and maybe call once in a while and… Why are you shaking your head?"

"I don't want to be without you for a year."

"You didn't even know me seven weeks ago!"

"And now I do, and I don't want to leave you, Molly. Come with me."

"What?"

"Come to England with me."

"I… I don't think I can. I promised my dad I'd start work at the store when I get home."

"Could you delay that for a year?"

"He's so excited about me starting. I just… I couldn't bear to disappoint him."

Linc thought about that for a second. "You want to know what I think we ought to do?"

She was almost afraid to ask. "What?"

"You should take me to Vermont to check out this country store your family owns and see if there might be a place for me there."

She stared at him as if he'd just suggested they take a quick trip to Venus. "Are you *out of your mind*? You have an MBA from *Yale*. What in the hell do you want with a country store in Vermont?"

"I'm intrigued, and by the way you described it, it sounds like something that would interest me."

"No."

"Just no? We're not even going to talk about it?"

"We did talk about it, and you're not doing that. It's insanity. You could do anything you want."

"Exactly—and what I want is to check out your family's business in Vermont."

41

"You're going to England."

"Maybe not." He reached for her, wrapped his arms around her and kissed her. "I love you. I don't want to be without you ever again. Even if that means living in Vermont and running a country store. I'd live in a tent if I got to be with you."

"The heat has pickled your brain. You're not thinking clearly."

"I've never thought more clearly than I am right now. I look at you, and I see everything I ever wanted."

"How can that be true?"

"I don't know. It just is." He kissed her again, more intently this time, as if trying to prove what he'd said was true.

She was beginning to believe him. "You're going to England."

"Maybe not."

"You're going."

"We'll see." Tipping his head for a better angle, he kissed her again.

They ended up reclined on her air mattress, oblivious to the intense heat or anything other than each other. They'd shared a few stolen kisses here and there before today, but with privacy hard to come by in the camp, it had never progressed beyond that. But this…

Molly was lost to him and how he made her feel. And knowing he loved her, as preposterous as that might seem, made being with him even more necessary to her. Her bikini top disappeared, and with her breasts pressed against his chest, the desire was dizzying.

And then she felt guilty. How could she be doing this with someone else when Andrew was gone forever? She broke the kiss and took a couple of deep breaths while berating herself for letting this thing with Lincoln get so out of hand.

"What's wrong?" He ran his thumb over her nipple, making her tremble.

"I… I can't do this."

"Why not?"

"I just can't." She pushed on his shoulder and sat up, reaching for a T-shirt and putting it on.

"Mol…"

"I'm going to take a shower before dinner." Molly grabbed her shower bag and left the tent before he could talk her into staying. She was beginning to realize he could talk her into just about anything.

CHAPTER FIVE

"Love one another."
—George Harrison

Molly avoided him for two very long days. At the end of the second day, they were wrapping up at the site when Keisha drove in, her car skidding to a stop before she got out and called for Joseph. The frantic edge to her voice put Linc immediately on alert.

Something was wrong.

Joseph came rushing out of the house where he'd been working.

Keisha ran over to him.

Linc could see she was crying.

"What's going on?" Charlie, one of the other volunteers, asked him.

"I don't know." Joseph and Keisha had become their friends, and Lincoln wanted to know what he could do to help them. He walked over to them. "Are you okay?"

The look of terror on Joseph's face sent a chill down Linc's spine. "Jalen has been arrested."

Jalen was their fourteen-year-old son, and he, too, had become a friend during the summer as he worked with them when he wasn't in summer school to catch up in math.

"For what?"

Keisha looked at him, eyes full of fear and anger. "For being Black."

Lincoln was taken aback, both by the vehemence in her tone and the terror coming from both of them.

"What do you know, honey?" Joseph asked, his voice tense.

Keisha wiped tears from her face. "He and two friends were walking in town after school let out, and according to the other boys, the police stopped them to find out where they were going. When they said they were going home, the police started asking them if they were part of a fight that happened last night. Jalen said they knew nothing about it. The police said they didn't like his attitude and cuffed him. When the other boys protested, they told them to shut up or they'd take them in, too."

"Let's go get him out," Joseph said.

"If we can do anything…" Linc said, feeling impotent, angry and scared for his friends.

"We'll be back," Joseph said. "Finish cleaning up, and call it a day." He got into the driver's side of Keisha's car, waited for her to get in and took off, leaving a cloud of dust behind him.

"Jesus," Cory said. "What the hell?"

"I don't know," Linc said, his stomach twisted in knots.

"It's not good," Desmond, who was one of Joseph's business partners, said. "Happens far too often, and sometimes it doesn't end well."

"How can they get away with that?" Charlie asked.

Desmond, who was also Black, shot him a withering look. "Get away with it? They're the police. They get away with whatever the fuck they want. Who's gonna stop them?"

"There has to be something we can do," Linc said.

"Do us all a favor and stay in your lane. This is so much bigger than you and one summer in Mississippi." Desmond walked away, got in his truck and drove off.

Linc hoped he was going to help Joseph and Keisha, because it seemed like they'd need all the help they could get.

"What's going on?" Molly asked when she walked over from one of the other houses.

Linc caught her up.

"Come on. No way. He's the best kid. They can't just do that."

"That's what we were just saying," Linc told her, "and apparently, they *can* do it. From what Desmond said, it happens far too often."

"That makes me sick," Molly said, folding her arms as if she needed a hug.

He understood how she felt.

Much later, they sat with a subdued group of volunteers in camp, wishing they could do something for Joseph and Keisha. But they'd done what had been requested of them and had stayed put while they prayed for Jalen and his family.

Linc gave Molly's hand a squeeze, got up from their gathering and walked away, needing a minute to himself. He stood by the tree line, staring into the darkness as despair seeped into his soul. Jalen was the best kid—fun, funny, talented at sports and music, an A student except for the math he struggled with, and respectful to his parents as well as the volunteers he worked with. The thought of anything happening to him, an innocent kid caught up in something so much bigger than him...

Then Molly was there, her arm around his waist and her head on his shoulder, and that was all it took for him to feel slightly better, to know she understood, that she felt the same way he did.

"It's so awful," she said softly.

"I wish there was something we could do."

"We can continue to support Joseph and his family and the other friends we've made here and come back next summer if they'll have us. We'll come as often as we can, and maybe, over time, we'll start to see things get better."

"I like that idea a lot."

Linc put his arm around her and held her close to him, needing to keep her there for a lot longer than this summer. "I'm not going to England, Mol."

"Yes, you are."

"No, I'm not."

"Yes."

"No."

"Yes."

He let her have the last word, but his mind was already made up. After spending this summer with her, the only thing he wanted was more of how he felt when she was in his arms.

"WHAT HAPPENED TO JALEN?" WILL ASKED.

"They released him two days later without charging him with anything."

"They didn't hurt him, did they?" Ella asked.

"Thankfully, they didn't, but it took a long time for their family to get past the incident. Keisha would tell you that Joseph was never quite the same afterward. But Jalen, he survived and thrived. He's an attorney now, working on behalf of Black men and women who are unjustly detained or incarcerated. He's made quite a name for himself."

"They came here," Hunter said. "I remember it."

"They did," Linc said. "You would've been about three or four. Jalen was looking at law schools up here and toured UVM. They stayed with us."

"I remember, too," Hannah said. "He pushed us on the swings. They had a daughter, too, right?"

Linc nodded. "Jasmine. She was three years younger than Jalen. She's an accountant and has three kids. We hear from them at Christmas, and I talk to Joseph at least once a month."

"We spent a second summer working with him." Molly snuggled Callie, who was sound asleep in her arms. "And made a lot of good friends over those summers. It was the most rewarding work we ever did. Joseph built almost three hundred homes, and we still support the foundation he started to help other first-time homeowners."

"And Dad didn't go to England," Max said.

"Not that fall, but I did get there eventually." He smiled at Molly. "Your mom planned a trip for our tenth anniversary. You older kids might remember how she took me on a Beatles tour. We went to Liverpool, Abbey Road, Eleanor Rigby's tombstone, Penny Lane and Strawberry Field, among other places. She was very thorough."

"I never wanted him to regret giving up that year in England for me."

"And I never did. Not for one second, as you know."

"Mom, what would you have done if he'd had to go to England?" Hunter asked.

"I suppose I would've gone with him, but I'd promised Gramps I'd come to work at the store when I got home from Mississippi. I didn't want to disappoint him, either."

"What I want to know is how you ended up in Vermont running Mom's family business," Will said. "Any time we've asked you about that, you've always said it was a long story that was better left untold."

"I still feel that way, but now I need to tell you because today I heard from my family for the first time since my father made me choose between him and your mother."

Charley gasped. "What? *Seriously?* He made you *choose?*"

"Very seriously," Linc said, gazing at Molly. "Of course, there was never any contest, but that was a terribly difficult time for us."

THE NIGHT BEFORE THEY WERE DUE TO BREAK CAMP AND HEAD home, Lincoln went looking for Molly. Since the camp wasn't very big, she shouldn't have been hard to find, but after he'd looked everywhere, he started asking the others where she was.

"She said something about going into town," one of the other volunteers said.

"By herself?" Ever since Jalen's arrest, he'd been more aware of the potential for trouble. Alarmed, Linc was running for his bike before their friend Gloria could finish confirming that Molly had gone into town by herself.

Just as he rounded the corner to head for town, he encountered Molly coming back and knew a moment of pure relief as he turned his bike to ride to camp with her.

"What're you doing out here?" she asked.

"Looking for you."

The rode back to camp together and stashed the bikes before going to sit inside Molly's tent. "What were you doing in town by yourself, sweetheart?" he asked.

"I wanted to buy you a present, but I couldn't find anything I liked."

"You don't have to get me anything."

"I wanted you to know how much I'm going to miss you."

His heart broke when he saw her subtly swipe at a tear. Linc put his arm around her and rested his chin on the top of her head. "You're not going to have to miss me. I'm going home to Vermont with you. I bought my bus ticket yesterday."

"You did not!"

"I did, too. I told you… My plans have changed. I want different things now."

"You can't. You'll regret not going to England."

He held her even closer. "The only thing I'd regret is letting you get away. I'm going to Vermont."

"You'll hate it there. You'll be so bored."

"Will you be there?"

"Yes, but—"

"No buts. If you're there, I'll never be bored." He pulled back from her, tipped her chin up and kissed the tears off her cheeks. "I swear to God I'll never regret not going to England, but I know for sure I'd always regret not going with you." Then he kissed her lips, lingering over the sweet, salty taste of her. "I really need you to believe me when I tell you I've fallen madly in love with you this summer, and any chance I have of being happy is all wrapped up in you now."

She wiped new tears from her face. "I'm still trying to figure out how that's possible."

"Have you met you? You're the best person I've ever known. Anyone would want to be with you."

"Do you promise you'll never blame me for giving up Oxford?"

"I promise."

"You're sure, Linc? Really, *really* sure about this?"

"Guess what?"

"What?"

"I love you more than the Beatles."

CHAPTER SIX

"Love is the answer, and you know that for sure; Love is a flower,
and you've got to let it grow."
—John Lennon

olly laughed as she subtly tended to the tears that came any time she recalled the most important moment of her life, when she knew for certain that Lincoln Abbott truly loved her. "That's what convinced me he was serious."

"Dad had some serious game," Hunter said. "I'm impressed."

"I was, too," Molly said. "When he said he'd never regret not going to England but would always regret not coming with me…" She fanned her face. "He definitely had me on the hook with that, but when he said he loved me more than the Beatles… There was no going back from that. Not that I wanted to."

"So, you guys left Mississippi and came to Vermont?" Wade asked.

"Yep," Linc said. "It was a thirty-hour bus ride that we

spent making plans. I'd find a job, we'd get a place to live, we'd figure out how soon we could get married and get busy having the babies your mother wanted."

"You never considered living anywhere else?" Landon asked.

"I knew from the way your mom talked about Vermont and her family that she wouldn't be happy living anywhere else, and since I'd never felt that way about anywhere I'd been or lived, I was fine with doing whatever it took to make her happy."

"You see why I fell madly in love?" Molly asked.

"This is heading into the TMI category," Charley said in her typically blunt way. "What I want to know is what happened when Dad told his father he wasn't going into the family business."

"We're getting to that," Linc said. "But before we do, we should tell you about the first time I came to Vermont and met your grandparents."

～

THE BUS RIDE WAS LONG, BUT BEING WITH LINC MADE IT MORE than tolerable. He was so full of excitement and plans for their future that Molly could hardly keep up with him. She still wanted to pinch herself that the kind, intelligent, incredibly sexy man she'd met in Mississippi loved her more than the Beatles and wanted to marry her as soon as possible.

Her head was spinning, but in the best possible way. His excitement was contagious, even if she still worried that someday he'd be sorry he'd given up the chance to live in his beloved England for a year. He'd promised he wouldn't, and she had no choice but to believe him, especially since he was making plans that required her full attention.

"I called a Realtor in Butler before we left Mississippi," he told her when they were outside of New York City.

"You did *what?*"

"I called a Realtor, told her how much I could afford to put down, and she found me what she called a fixer-upper. We can use everything we learned this summer to make it our own."

"You did not buy property without even seeing it first."

"What if I did?"

"Lincoln! You're *insane!* No one does that. And when were you going to tell me about it? We've been on this bus for more than twenty hours already!"

"People do things like that when they're trying to convince the one they love that they're serious about making a life in the place she loves."

"You told me you love me more than the Beatles. I'm already convinced you're serious."

"We're going to need a place to live."

"So you wait until we get there to figure that out. You don't call some random Realtor who might be a scammer for all you know. Who is it anyway?"

"Someone named Gertrude who goes by the nickname of Dude."

Molly began to laugh. She laughed so hard she couldn't breathe.

"What's so funny?"

"You bought a house from the woman known in town as Snow White because all she really cares about is animals."

"Oh."

"Yeah. What the heck did she sell you?"

"Now, don't freak out or anything…"

"Oh my God. *What did you do?*"

"She told me about a barn on Hells Peak Road. You know that road?"

Again, Molly laughed until she cried. She laughed so hard, she ended up in a coughing fit. "Tell me," she said between gasping breaths that had the few other people on the bus staring at them, "that you didn't buy the old Andersen barn."

"I'm not sure who the current owners are," Linc said, a bit indignantly.

"You have no idea what you bought, do you?"

"I bought us a place to live."

"You bought us a falling-down wreck of a barn where cows were living a few months ago!"

"She said it was the only property currently for sale in Butler, but she didn't mention the cows."

"Why am I not surprised?"

"Is this woman named Dude an actual Realtor?"

"Among other things. It's okay. You can get the money back, right?"

"Um, well, so..."

"Lincoln Abbott! *You did not put down money you can't get back on a falling-down wreck of a barn where cows lived a few months ago!*" She paused, looked at him, her eyes wide with alarm. "*Did you?*"

"Maybe?" he said with a sheepish grin.

"How much?"

"Like ten thousand?"

"*Dollars?*"

"Yes, dollars, and don't look at me that way. If I want your parents to take me seriously as their daughter's future husband, we needed a place to live."

"Did it have to be a falling-down barn where cows lived a few months ago?"

"It needed to have room for all the kids you told me you wanted."

"At least they'll each have their own stall. Will they get fresh hay every day, too?"

Linc gave her the side-eye. "I had no idea that my sweet Molly Stillman could be so sarcastic."

"Still want to give up Oxford to live in a broken-down barn in Vermont that probably smells like cow shit?"

"Hell yes, because sarcastic Molly is sexy Molly."

"You're not right in the head."

"I believe I told you that the night we met when you called me a sociopath."

"I should've paid closer attention that night. What else did Dude sell you besides a broken-down barn with a sagging roof?"

"She sold me on a dream of a life in Butler, Vermont, with you and our stable full of kids and maybe your family's business if your dad decides to hire me, and snowy winters and breathtaking autumns, of apple picking and maple-syrup making and a simple, fulfilling life that sounds better to me than anything I've ever experienced. But only if you're there to make it all perfect."

"I'm thinking about forgiving you for the barn. Eventually."

"When that barn is the coolest house in Butler, you'll be thanking me for having the foresight and wisdom to get us a home that can accommodate the five children you told me you want."

"*Five?* I said maybe three."

"I heard five."

"Now you're hearing things, too. I'm starting to seriously question my choices where you're concerned."

"You're not really, are you?"

"No, but I'm not having five children."

"Four, then."

"Three."

"Maybe we'll get lucky with twins."

"I'll kill you if that happens."

"No, you won't. You love me too much to kill me."

"If you knock me up with twins, I will kill you. Stand warned."

"Good to know. I'll tell my boys to focus on one egg at a time."

"You do that."

"How soon can we do that? All this talk about eggs is making me hot."

Molly giggled when he kissed her neck and made her shiver. "Soon. I promise."

With almost no privacy in the camp, they'd had to put their ardor on ice until they could be alone somewhere. And there was something she still needed to share with him that she hadn't yet. Not because she didn't think he'd understand, but because it was still too painful to talk about, even with him.

"So my dad will probably meet us at the bus station, and he's kind of weird about me and my sister, Hannah, when it comes to boys and dating and stuff."

"Weird how?"

"Weird in that he'd rather we didn't date or speak to boys at all if possible."

"He knows that's ridiculous, right?"

"Of course he does, but you have to kind of ease him into the whole 'Molly has a boyfriend' thing. Let him get to know you a little before you let on that we're, you know…"

"Dying to have sex?"

"Lincoln! *Stop.*"

He absolutely loved the way her entire complexion lit up when she was embarrassed. That made embarrassing her some of the best fun he'd ever had. "Are we or are we not dying to have sex?"

"If you say that again, you'll never have it with me."

"Have what? Say it."

"I won't say it, and neither will you if you know what's good for you."

"I know what's good for me," he said, nuzzling her neck again, "and her name is Molly. Sweet, sweet Molly. I can't wait until we can sleep naked together every night."

"*Stop.*"

"I'll never stop wanting that. When we're old and gray, I'll still want to sleep naked with you."

"My advice would be not to mention anything about that when you're within five hundred miles of my father, or it may never happen."

"Good to know."

"He's a really, really good guy, and you'll love him once we get past the initial awkwardness of him realizing I met a guy who wants to marry me and have babies with me. Maybe don't mention babies until we're safely married."

"Got it. Anything else?"

"Keep your hands to yourself when he's around, or you might lose one of them."

"Also good to know. Please tell me your mother is normal."

"She's the sweetest person you'll ever meet, and he is, too. After you get to know him."

"I'll take your word on that."

"You'll see. He'll come around. It just might take him a minute or two to decide he can trust you."

They sat with their heads together, hands clasped, and dozed during the final stretch of the seemingly endless trip. By the time they pulled into the station in Rutland, Linc was more than ready to get off that bus and check out his new home state of Vermont. As he made his plans with Molly, he still had things to contend with at home in Philadelphia. But he would deal with that after he put the pieces together in Vermont.

Step one was meeting Molly's parents and convincing them he would love and care for their daughter for the rest of his life. Step two was finding a job, and step three would be proposing to her and setting a wedding date. After all that was done, he'd take his new fiancée home to Philadelphia to meet his family and share their plans.

Elmer Stillman was waiting for them at the bus station.

Molly let out a happy cry and leaped into her father's outstretched arms.

"You can't ever leave me for that long again," Elmer said as he hugged her.

"Don't be dramatic, Daddy."

"I'm not being dramatic. Longest summer of my life, hands down. Counting the days until my little girl came home."

"I'm going to be twenty-three soon. When will you stop referring to me as your little girl?"

"When I'm dead and buried?" He took one of her bags, grabbed her hand and headed for the parking lot.

"Wait, Dad. I brought home a friend who I want you to meet and be nice to."

Elmer stopped, dropped her hand and turned, noticing Linc for the first time and eyeing him suspiciously.

"Hello, sir, I'm Lincoln Abbott, a friend of Molly's."

Elmer shook his hand but continued to size him up with sharp blue eyes that made Lincoln feel like a little boy. "What kind of friend are you, son?"

"The boyfriend kind, sir."

"Is that right?"

Lincoln refused to be the first one to blink. "Yes, sir. I love your daughter very much, and I hope to marry her as soon as possible."

"Linc! I told you to *ease him in*. That doesn't count as *easing him in*!"

Elmer scowled fiercely. "My Molly doesn't have boyfriends."

"Honestly, Dad, I've had a boyfriend before, as you well know, so stop acting like a fool and be nice to my new friend."

"Is he your friend or your *boy*friend?"

"Um, well..."

Linc nudged her and gave her an annoyed look.

"Boyfriend. He's definitely my boyfriend."

"Who wants to marry you," Elmer said, giving Linc another suspicious glare.

"That's what he says."

"You two do know I can hear you talking about me, right?" Linc asked.

Elmer sent him a withering look that made Linc thankful looks couldn't actually kill. "No one is talking to you." To Molly, Elmer said, "Where is *he* staying?"

"With us, Dad. Now stop acting like a Neanderthal and take me home to see Mom and Hannah." Molly took her father by the arm and pulled him along with her as they headed out of the bus station.

Lincoln followed, hoping Elmer would let him into the car.

❧

"I DECIDED RIGHT THEN AND THERE THAT IF I EVER HAD daughters, I wouldn't act the fool with the men they brought home," Linc said. "I'd be much more evolved than Elmer was, that was for sure."

Hannah, Ella and Charley lost it laughing when they heard that.

"What*ever*," Charley said. "You were the biggest ass-pain in history when we started dating."

"Remember how he'd never let Caleb and me be in the same room by ourselves, even if we were just watching TV?" Hannah asked.

"I remember that," Hunter said, laughing. "He'd sit between you on the sofa."

"It was outrageous!" Hannah said. "Even when we were *engaged*, he was ridiculous."

"My father-in-law taught me everything I know about keeping my daughters away from scheming young men," Linc said, amused by their memories. He'd discovered some promises to himself were easier to keep than others, such as when boys had begun sniffing around his three precious daughters. Like Elmer, he'd been a little over the top, not that he'd ever admit that to his girls.

"I had your number from the second you stepped off that bus," Elmer said. "Imagine showing up out of the blue and talking about *marrying* my Molly. You were out of your mind."

"I was madly in love," Linc said with a smile for his beloved.

"It was revolting," Elmer said, making his grandchildren howl with laughter.

Molly reached for Linc's hand. "Nothing revolting about it, and you have to admit, Dad, he jumped through all your ridiculous hoops."

"He did," Elmer conceded. "Even the ones I thought would trip him up."

"Like when he sat outside your mother's bedroom all night the first night I stayed at their house to make sure I wouldn't wander during the night," Linc said.

"How did you know I was there if you didn't wander?" Elmer asked, raising a brow.

"I refuse to answer that question on the grounds that

there's no statute of limitations on crimes committed while in the throes of forever love."

"Barf," Landon said.

"Nothing to barf about, son," Linc replied. "Your mother was and is a beautiful woman. I wanted to be with her all the time. Still do."

"And I knew that the second I saw the way you looked at my little girl," Elmer said.

"Your *little girl* was almost twenty-three."

"She's *still* my little girl, even after you had ten children with her. It would do you well not to forget that, young man."

"I never do, sir."

Elmer's smile lit up his adorable face. Despite their auspicious—and suspicious—beginning, Linc and his father-in-law were the best of friends. They spent part of just about every day together, even if it was over a cup of coffee at the diner, during which they usually did nothing but push each other's buttons. He'd learned everything he knew about being a good husband and father from Elmer and turned to him any time his heart was heavy, including now.

"What did you think of Butler when you first came, Dad?" Will asked.

"I loved it immediately, especially the store. I'd never seen anything quite like it."

"I decided to hire him so I could keep an eye on him," Elmer said.

"Oh, *puleeze*," Linc said. "You were lusting after my Yale MBA. Admit it."

"I'll admit no such thing, but I will give you credit for growing the business in ways I never dreamed possible."

"Thanks to my Yale MBA."

"Oh, stuff it."

"Do you kids see what I had to put up with from your grandfather from the very beginning?" Linc asked.

"Seems to me he kept you humble," Hannah said.

"Exactly, sweetheart," Elmer said. "He needed to eat some humble pie when he got here all high off his new Ivy League MBA, telling me he was going to *marry* my Molly. The impertinence."

Molly laughed at the face her father made. "It's been forty years, Dad. It might be time to move on."

"Never."

"Why did you hire him if you were so suspicious of him, Gramps?" Ella asked.

"You know that saying, keep your friends close and your enemies closer?" Elmer asked, giving Linc a calculating look.

"Which was Dad?" Ella asked.

"I didn't know yet, so I figured if I hired him, I could keep an eye on him and figure out which he was going to be."

"Oh what*ever*," Linc said. "You were *drooling* over my MBA."

"That was vomit over the way you mooned after my daughter."

"I never once mooned your daughter."

"Well," Molly said, "there was that one time—"

"Say another word, and I'll fire him," Elmer said as the others laughed.

As the chairman of the company's board of directors, Elmer could, in fact, fire him, not that he ever would. Linc had done a good job of growing Elmer's family business from a small-town store into a brand that was beginning to gain national recognition.

"What I want to know," Will said, "is what your dad said when you told him you'd accepted a job working for a country store in Vermont."

"Yeah, that didn't go so well," Linc said, sagging a bit when he recalled the reason he was reliving some things he'd much rather forget.

"Let me," Molly said, tuning in to him as always.

"Sure, love. Go ahead."

"About a month after your dad came home to Vermont with me, we went hiking on the mountain one day. It was a clear, cool beautiful September day, and when we reached the summit, he dropped to one knee and proposed. Even though I knew it was coming, he still took me by surprise that day, which I consider one of the best days of my life."

"Were you still worried about him giving up Oxford?" Charley asked.

"A little, but he seemed really happy working at the store and living in Butler. We'd begun work on the barn, with a goal of having a bedroom, kitchen and bathroom habitable by the time the winter came along. The mudroom was our first bedroom."

"I thought you always joked we were conceived in a tent," Hunter said, frowning. "As if we needed to know that."

"You were," Molly said, "but that's not part of the story you need to hear."

"Thank you, Jesus," Colton said. "Ain't no one wants to hear that."

"It's a pretty good story," Molly said with a saucy grin for Linc.

"*No!*" their ten children said as one, with Elmer joining in the chorus.

"It's not too late for me to run that boyfriend of yours out of town on a rail," Elmer said.

"Actually, Dad, it's about ten kids too late. But anyway, where was I? Oh yes, so we're engaged and working on the barn, and Dad is enjoying working for Gramps, even if Gramps threatens to kill him on a daily basis."

"That was a very dangerous time in my life," Linc said with a wry grin, "but well worth the danger to be with my Mols every day."

"The only thing standing between us and our plans was the fact that your father hadn't told his family he'd decided to live and work in Vermont rather than go to England. And he wasn't going to work for his family's business."

"Where did they think you were the whole time you were in Vermont?"

"At Oxford."

"You would've killed us if we'd done something like that," Charley said.

"Oh, absolutely," Linc said. "I'm not saying it was the right thing to do, but I wanted to have my life in Vermont set up before I went home to tell them my plans had changed. And I wanted your mom and me to be engaged."

"Did he ask for her hand, Gramps?" Will asked.

"He did, and he said all the right things about how he'd take care of her and protect her and love her for the rest of his life. However, there was no mention of ten children, or I might've had to think twice."

"But then you wouldn't have us," Max said, gesturing to himself, Lucas and Landon, the youngest three siblings.

"And that would've been a tragedy for sure. I've put up with *him* because I got all of you."

"Which is why the two of you have been scheming for years to get us all paired off," Ella said with a kind smile for her grandfather. "Because you can barely tolerate him."

"Exactly. As soon as you kids are all happily settled, I can be done with him once and for all. Impertinent upstart, showing up holding hands with *my* Molly like he has a right to hold her hand."

"He did have a right, Dad, so you can knock off that tired forty-year-old nonsense."

Her father smiled sweetly at her. "What fun would that be, my dear?"

Molly rolled her eyes at her father. "I insisted we go to see his family when we set a wedding date."

"I didn't want to go," Linc said. "I was afraid they'd find a way to mess with the perfection I'd found with your mother."

"Were they unkind?" Hannah asked, her brows furrowing as if she couldn't imagine parents being unkind to their own child.

"It wasn't that so much as my father had a vision for how we ought to live our lives, and if we stepped outside the lines, he was quick to set us straight. It'd always been that way, and it had gotten much worse after we lost Hunter, so I had to believe it would be even more so in this case. And unfortunately, I was right."

CHAPTER SEVEN

"Time you enjoy wasting was not wasted."
—John Lennon

$\mathcal{L}$inc had lived in a blissful state of denial for more than two months by the time Molly insisted they take a trip to Philadelphia so she could meet his family and they could share their plans with them. He'd taken to life in Butler, Vermont, like the proverbial fish to water. He loved everything about small-town living—the ability to walk to just about anywhere, the friendly people, the charming store that Molly's family ran and, of course, Molly herself.

If she'd been lovely in Mississippi, she was even more so in her hometown, surrounded by her beloved family and friends. After being there with her, he could plainly see that she wouldn't be content anywhere else. She had the same desire to travel and see the world that he had, but her home and her heart would always be in Vermont.

Before he met her, he would've wondered if he could be

satisfied living in a small town like Butler, but if she was nearby, he had what he needed. It was really that simple. And he loved working with her dad, even if he still treated him with the same suspicion he might bestow upon a serial killer who'd expressed an interest in dating his daughter.

Linc was able to see through the bluster. He respected Elmer for being concerned about the man in his daughter's life, but he was determined to prove he had nothing to worry about where Linc was concerned. Linc wanted the same thing Elmer did—for Molly to be safe, happy and loved for the rest of her life. He was more than prepared to live up to his end of that bargain, if only the showdown with his own family didn't loom so large, like a black cloud hanging over his happily ever after.

"I'm sure that once they see we're truly in love, they'll be supportive," Molly said as they worked late into the night at the barn in early October.

They planned to get married in January, after the holiday rush at the store, and he was counting the days until she was his wife. He couldn't wait to sleep with her in his arms every night for the rest of his life. The time they spent at their future home filled him with anticipation for when they'd finally be living there together, rather than sleeping separately at her parents' home, where he'd been relegated to the basement. He'd been tempted to sneak upstairs, but after Elmer had staked out Molly's room that first night and later shown him his hunting rifle, he'd chosen to stay put, which, of course, had been Elmer's goal.

But here at the barn, they were completely alone, and even though they had more work to do than they could complete in a year, all he wanted was to be with her.

"I wish I was so certain," Linc said. "Of course they'll love you. Who wouldn't? But they won't be happy that I plan to live here rather than there. That doesn't fit with their idea of how my life should unfold."

"We're planning a wedding that's a couple of months away, and your parents don't even know about me. I don't feel right about that."

He didn't either. If only he wasn't so afraid they were going to somehow ruin the best thing to ever happen to him.

"We'll drive to Philly this weekend and get it taken care of. They have a right to know you're getting married, Linc."

"I guess."

She sat on the floor of the room that would serve as their temporary bedroom while they worked on what would eventually be a two-story dwelling with plenty of bedrooms, painting the trim they'd installed over the weekend. Their summer in Mississippi had prepared them well for the challenges they faced at the barn he'd bought sight unseen that did, in fact, still bear the faint aroma of cow shit.

Throughout those early months in Vermont, he'd known in the back of his mind that he needed to take steps that would bind him to his new life before he told his parents about the change in direction his life had taken. Their engagement, his job and the purchase of the barn had been critical to that plan.

"I can't believe they've thought you were in England all this time. It's not right that you haven't told them where you really are. My parents would lose their shit if I did that."

He squatted behind her, moved her ponytail out of the way and nuzzled her neck, making her giggle.

"Linc! Stop. I'm painting."

"Take a break. I want to show you something."

"Let me just finish this section."

He waited, not so patiently, for her to be done and then helped her up from the floor. "I hope you're not regretting choosing me, since you're having to spend every night working over here after working all day."

"Are you kidding? I love that we're doing this ourselves. Imagine how proud of it we'll be when it's finished."

"If it's ever finished." The enormity of the task they'd taken on overwhelmed him at times, but she was completely unfazed.

"It will be, and people will come from all over to see our amazing home."

He took her hand and led her outside, where the air had become crisp and chilly as September had faded into October. The fall colors had dazzled him as he'd been introduced to an entirely new pastime called "leaf peeping." According to Elmer, peeping season was the store's busiest time of year—even more so than Christmas—and he was seeing that for himself as the autumn colors headed toward a spectacular peak.

"Where're we going?" Molly asked as they trekked across their huge backyard.

"Follow me, and you shall see."

"You're being very mysterious."

Smiling, he led her through the inky darkness to the place he'd set up for them earlier. "I wanted to take you somewhere romantic, somewhere we could be alone, but I kept coming back to our own home." He pulled out the flashlight he'd stashed in his coat pocket earlier and illuminated the tent he'd pitched.

"What do you have in mind?" she asked with a small, sexy smile.

"You know what I have in mind."

"I thought we were going to wait."

"I can't wait. It's all I think about. *You're* all I think about. I can't work or think or function, because all I want is to be with you. You've completely bewitched me."

"I see the way you look at me in the office," she said, stepping closer to him.

"How do I look at you?"

"Like you want to carry me out of there and have your wicked way with me."

"That's about right."

"You're a terrible distraction."

"Am I?"

"You know you are."

He held the tent flap for her, and she went in ahead of him to find the bed he'd made for them from an air mattress, sheets and a quilt he'd bought at the store two days ago, after Elmer had left for the day. Linc suspected his future father-in-law probably knew about the purchase, even though he hadn't been there.

"This is lovely," Molly said, sitting on the bed.

"No, it isn't, but it's all ours, with no rifles around for miles. Or so I hope." Elmer had been rather quiet about them working at the barn late into the night. Linc suspected that was because his sweet wife, Sarah, had told Elmer to leave them alone. Molly's mother had been nothing but warm and welcoming to Linc, and he would love her forever for that.

"It's lovely because you did this for us."

"I'm a selfish asshole because all I want in this entire world is to make love with you."

"I want that, too."

"You do?"

"Lincoln," she said, laughing. "For someone so smart, you can be awfully dumb at times."

"Hey!" He came down next to her, landing hard enough to bounce her and take full advantage of her being off-balance to arrange himself on top of her. "Hi."

"Hi."

"I can't believe you're being mean to me when I went to all this trouble to get you alone in the dark."

"I'm not being mean. I'm laughing at you. Two very different things."

"I'd much rather you use that sassy mouth to kiss me."

"Before I do that, there's something I need to tell you... Something I should've told you before now."

The sadness and reluctance he heard in her tone put him on guard. He didn't want to hear anything that would upset either of them. Not now, anyway. "What's on your mind?"

"I... It's something I don't really talk about because it's so painful."

Linc moved so he was next to her, on his side facing her. The flashlight he'd left on made it so he could see the furrow of her brows and an expression on her face he hadn't seen before. It looked a lot like grief. He cupped her cheek and ran his thumb over her soft skin. "You don't have to tell me if it hurts too much."

"I do have to tell you, and it's not that I haven't wanted to before now. It's just that some things are almost unbearable."

"I hate that something ever hurt you that way."

"My mom says it's the price you pay for loving someone, and I loved Andrew, from the time I was in seventh grade until he died our junior year of high school."

"Oh God, Mol. I'm so sorry. What happened to him?"

"He was diagnosed with bone cancer in ninth grade. He fought it hard, and when we realized he was going to die... I, we, well..."

"You don't have to say it. I get it."

"I feel guilty that I've led you to believe I've never done it before."

"I'm glad you got to have that experience with him, but I'm so sorry you lost him."

"It's the worst thing I've ever been through. I wanted to

die myself for a while afterward, but over time, I got past those feelings and started to get back to living. I still feel guilty sometimes that I'm alive when he isn't, and when I first met you, I felt super guilty for having those feelings for someone else. That night in Mississippi when we were kissing, and I said I couldn't..."

"I understand, and nothing has to happen between us until you want it to. I want you to be comfortable."

"I'm so comfortable with you. The way I was with him, and I didn't think that would ever happen again. You have no idea what a relief it's been to know that I *can* feel that way for someone else, even if I'll always miss him."

"I'm glad you feel that way with me. I want you to be comfortable and happy."

"I love you so much, Linc." Her eyes sparkled with unshed tears. "You can't possibly know what you've done for me since we met. You've made me feel hopeful and excited when I worried for the longest time after Andrew died that I'd never feel that way again. I hadn't dated anyone since I lost him."

"I'm honored to be the first one you've dated since you lost him." He wiped away her tears and tucked a strand of hair behind her ear. "Is that why your dad has been so suspicious of me?"

She laughed. "Partly, but he acted that way with Andrew, too. I think he's actually relieved to see me moving on after that terrible heartache. Anyway, he's all bark and no bite."

"He showed me his hunting rifle, Molly."

As she collapsed into helpless laughter, he decided he much preferred that to the sadness she'd shown him when she talked about her lost love. And then she reached for him, and he wasn't thinking about sadness or anything other than the way her lips moved under his, the way her body felt pressed up against him and how badly he wanted her.

~

"STOP." WILL HELD UP A HAND. "I SPEAK FOR ALL MY SIBLINGS when I say we do not want to know what went on in that tent."

"I do have one question," Hunter said.

"What's that?" Linc asked as the others covered their ears.

"You were married for a year or so when we were born, yet you always said Hannah and I were conceived in a tent. Weren't you living in the barn by then?"

"We were, but every dime we had was tied up in the barn, so other than the second summer we spent in Mississippi when your mom was expecting you guys, we took 'vacations' to our own backyard."

"That's so weird," Colton said.

"It was fun," Linc said, waggling his brows.

"Lots of fun," Molly added, smiling.

"And the best part was she didn't actually kill me when we found out she was expecting twins."

"That must've been a shock," Ella said, smiling.

"We laughed so much about how I doomed myself with that conversation on the bus," Molly said. "And we laughed some more when we found out we were having twins *again* with the boys."

Linc flexed his bicep. "She loved me too much to kill me. In fact—"

"Enough," Will said emphatically. "Tell us about going to Philly and what happened when you got there."

Linc's heart sank when he recalled that trip, not to mention the reason this had come up again. He still had to decide if he was going to see his father.

"We drove to Philadelphia the following weekend," Molly said.

"They must've been surprised to see you since they

thought you were in England," Charley said. "And again, I say you would've lost your shit if we did what you did."

"They were, and yes, I would have," Linc said. "My father was immediately suspicious and unfriendly to your mother. It was like he knew right away he wasn't going to like what I'd come there to tell him—and he took it out on her, acting as if she wasn't there."

"Ugh," Ella said. "That must've been awful."

"It was," Linc said, "but it only cemented my resolve. We met with my parents in my dad's study. He wanted to know why I wasn't in England. I looked at your mom, and I said because I've met the woman I'm going to marry."

FOR THE LONGEST TIME AFTER LINC SAID THOSE WORDS, THERE was only silence until his father spoke up. "You were hell-bent on spending a year in England, and we accommodated that request by shuffling the executive team around to cover for you. And now you tell me you've given that up for a *woman?*"

"That woman is my fiancée, Father, and I expect you to show her the respect she deserves."

"I mean no disrespect to her," Carlton Abbott said. "But this is absurd, Lincoln. You dramatically change your plans and don't even see fit to tell us?"

"I am telling you. I'm telling you now."

"Could we have a word in private with our son, please?" Carlton asked Molly.

Linc tightened his grip on her hand. "Anything you have to say to me can be said in front of her."

"This is ridiculous. You come home from a summer volunteering at some do-gooder project in Mississippi and tell us you're engaged and have given up your plan to study at Oxford, which was the only thing you wanted a few short months ago."

"Things change. I met Molly, and now I want different things."

"What different things do you want?"

"I want her, and… you should know, I've accepted a job with her family business in Vermont."

His father's complexion turned a worrisome shade of purple. "And what business is that?"

"It's a retail outfit."

"A retail outfit. In Vermont. Well, son, I have to give you credit. Your judgment is, as always, questionable at best."

"How can you say that? I've done everything you asked of me. I went to Yale because that's where you went. I got an MBA because that's what you wanted me to do. The first time I do something *I want*, you say my judgment is flawed? My judgment is just fine. I love Molly. I'm going to marry her and live in Vermont and work for her family's business, where I'll be free to think for myself."

"Is that what you think is going to happen?" Carlton asked with a mean sneer.

"It's already happened. I've been working there for two months already, and we bought a house."

"You bought a house. With whose money?"

"My money."

"Ah, the money your grandfather left you, I presume. If I recall correctly, you used a big chunk of that to pay for the year in England that's not going to happen now. Between that and the house you bought, you must be running kind of low, especially since you didn't work over the summer."

That was actually true, not that Linc would ever admit as much to his father.

"If you do this, if you walk away from your obligations to

this family and our business, that's the last money you'll ever see from this family."

"Carlton!" Linc's mother finally spoke up.

"Hush, Janet. This is between my son and me."

"Not if you're talking about cutting him off, it isn't."

"That's exactly what I'm talking about." To Linc, he said, "If you turn your back on this family, this family will turn its back on you."

His mother gasped. "Stop this right now, Carlton!"

"Shut your mouth!" Carlton's thundering shout had both women flinching.

Holding Molly's hand, Linc stood. "Come on, Mol. Let's go."

"If you walk out of here, you'll never hear from any of us again."

"If that's how you want it, Father, then so be it."

"Linc, wait," Molly said. "Surely you don't mean that. Neither of you means what you're saying."

"I do," Carlton said. "He made promises to me and this family, and I expect him to live up to them."

"Why would you want a son working for you who doesn't want to be there?"

"Since when do you not want to be there? That's been the plan for years!"

"That's been *your* plan. I never had a say in any of it. Hunter died, and suddenly my life belonged to you? I never signed on for that."

The mention of his late brother caused both his parents to flinch, and he immediately regretted bringing him into this.

"You didn't have any problem fully enjoying the lifestyle my company provided for you."

"What does that even mean?"

"The country club, the cars, the trips, college, grad school, all of it. You didn't mind any of that."

"I've always thanked you for anything you did for me. I'm not sure what else you expected."

"I expected my son to *care* about his legacy, to honor his commitments."

"And if I want something different for myself, you're going to make me choose?"

"Carlton, please," Janet said as tears filled her eyes. "Please don't do this."

"I haven't done anything but offer him a lifetime of luxury and security in a business he can walk right into."

"That's not what I want. I've never wanted it. I'm sorry I can't be what my brother was, but your dream has never been my dream."

Carlton's expression was positively murderous. "You ungrateful little brat."

"I'm not ungrateful, Father. I'm just not interested in working for you. I'm sorry if that hurts your feelings, but I'm not going to change my mind." He dropped a copy of the wedding invitation he'd brought on the coffee table in front of his mother. "Our wedding is in January. I hope to see you all there." He glanced at Molly, undone by her big eyes and pale face, and headed for the door, eager to get them both out of there.

"If you walk out of here, don't come back. You'll never hear from any of us again."

"Carlton! Stop this right now!"

"I mean it, Lincoln. If you leave, stay gone. The locks will be changed, and you'll be dead to this entire family."

Lincoln didn't believe him. There was no way his mother and siblings would go along with such an edict. "I'm sorry you can't be happy for me, Father. Mama, I love you. I'll always love you and the others. I'll make sure you know how to reach me."

He left the study and stopped short at the sight of his sister, Charlotte, and brother Max standing outside the door, the two of them teary-eyed and shocked.

"You heard that, I guess. This is Molly, my fiancée. Mol, my sister, Charlotte, and my brother Max."

"Linc..."

He stepped into Charlotte's outstretched arms.

"Don't go."

"I have to, but I'll write to you, and you can visit me in Vermont."

Charlotte clung to him, as if maybe she knew they'd never see each other again. He didn't believe that. Not then, anyway.

"We have to go. I'll be in touch."

"He doesn't mean it, Linc," Max said when he hugged him.

"Yeah, he does, but it'll be okay. Don't worry about me. I'll see you soon, all right?"

Max nodded tentatively, while Charlotte wept.

"He's being so unfair," Charlotte whispered.

He kissed her forehead. "Don't go to battle for me. Take care of yourselves and Will. Tell him I'll talk to him soon." Then he headed for the door without ever looking back. His life wasn't in this house. It was with the woman of his dreams in a broken-down barn that smelled like cow shit in Vermont.

"Linc, wait," Molly said when they were outside in the cool autumn air. "You can't leave it like this. You have to talk to him some more."

"It's not going to matter. His mind is made up, and he isn't going to change it. He forced me to choose, and I choose you. I choose you today, tomorrow and every day for the rest of my life."

"I… I just don't feel right about this. I don't want to be the reason for a rift in your family."

"You're not the reason, sweetheart." They stood next to Molly's old Toyota. "Why do you think I waited so long to come here? I knew how it would go. I didn't expect him to tell me I'd never see him again if I chose you and Vermont over him, but I knew he'd blow his top. I didn't want to deal with that, so I put it off. My only regret is that I brought you with me. I should've come alone so he couldn't treat you that way. I'm sorry for that."

"You have nothing to be sorry about, but really, Linc… You should go back in there by yourself and try to work this out."

"It won't matter. He's made up his mind, and I've made up mine. Let's go home."

"Wait."

He stopped, turned to her and looked down at her sweet face as she took a minute to decide what she wanted to say.

"I love you, Linc. You know I do. And I love the way you've changed your entire plan to make your life fit with mine, but this…" She glanced at the imposing red brick house with the black shutters and white pillars where he'd spent his childhood. "This is too much. You shouldn't have to give up everyone else you love to be with me."

Linc framed her face with his hands, compelling her to look at him with eyes that swam with tears he deeply resented. His father had made her cry. He'd never forgive him for that. "I need you to really hear me when I tell you there is nothing or no one that I want or need more than I want and need you. If I have you, I'll have everything. He forced me to choose, but there was never any choice to make. I choose you. Every day for the rest of my life. I choose you, Molly."

Tears spilled down her cheeks. "I don't want you to resent me for all the things you had to give up to have me."

"I never will. I swear to you, I'll never have a second of regret."

He put his arms around her and held her close, fully aware they were probably being watched from inside the house. *Good*, he thought. *Let them see how much I love her.* "Let's go home, sweetheart."

CHAPTER EIGHT

"The more I see, the less I know for sure."
—John Lennon

"And you never spoke to any of them ever again?" Hunter asked, incredulous.

"Nope," Linc said. "You have to remember those were different times. There were no cell phones or email or social media. I wrote to my mother and siblings every month, but they never once replied to me. I found out my mother died a few years ago when I got a letter from my father's attorney."

"Daddy," Ella said, tearful as she moved to hug him. "I'm so sorry they did that to you."

He held her close. "Thank you, love, but I've never been sorry that I chose your mom and our life here. Like I told Mom that day, I haven't had a single second of regret, even if I missed them. Of course I did."

"Have you tried to contact your siblings separate of your parents?" Will asked.

"I have," Linc said as he released Ella. "And never heard back. Until today."

"What happened today?" Hannah asked.

Linc could see from the haunted way his children looked at him that his story had touched them deeply, which didn't surprise him. They couldn't imagine losing each other the way he'd lost his family. "My sister, Charlotte, called to tell me my father is dying and wants to see me."

"No way," Colton said fiercely. "No fucking way are you doing that."

His son's strong reaction didn't surprise Linc. He felt the same way himself. To a point. "I understand why you'd say that, son, but I haven't decided either way yet. I wanted to talk to you kids about it before I made up my mind."

"How do you feel, Dad?" Hannah gave Colton a quelling look. "What do *you* want to do?"

"Part of me feels the way Colton does, but the other part, the part that's missed my original family so much over the years, is thinking about going."

"You know you don't have to, right?" Lucas asked. "If you decide not to go, you'd have no reason to feel guilty or anything like that. Tell me you know that."

"I do, son. I don't feel like I owe any of them anything. After all, they've known where I was all this time. They could've sought me out, but they chose not to for whatever reason. That's on them, not me."

"Do you *want* to go, Dad?" Wade asked.

"Part of me is curious about why my father wants to see me, and the chance to see Charlotte and my brothers is tempting. I can't deny that."

"If you go," Hunter said with a fierce edge to his voice, "we'll all go with you. Let them see what came of this choice they forced you to make."

"You don't have to do that. It's four days before Christmas. You're all busy at the store and with your own families."

"Try to stop us," Will said with the same fierceness his older brother had displayed.

"We'd never let you do this without us," Hannah said. "If you go, we all go."

The others nodded in agreement that brought tears to Linc's eyes. "If you wonder why I've never regretted my choices, it's because of you guys. All of you. I'm so proud of this family your mom and I built and the people you've grown up to be."

"I'm going, too," Elmer said. "I want them to see you had a father after yours turned his back on you."

Linc smiled at his father-in-law, touched by his support. "Thank you."

"Did you know what'd happened with Dad's family, Gramps?" Landon asked.

"I did know, and it was horrifying to me. I can't for the life of me imagine asking my kids to choose between me and the ones they loved."

"Even if you gave the man I love a run for his money at first," Molly said with a grin for her father. "And threatened him with a hunting rifle."

"I couldn't make it too easy on him," Elmer said.

"Mission accomplished," Linc said.

"This is why," Hunter said, "you made us all work somewhere else when we were in high school and college before we could come into the business. Isn't it?"

"It is," Linc said. "I wanted to make sure the choice to work for the family business was entirely yours and not something that felt like an obligation."

"He was very insistent on that," Elmer said.

"And we never knew why until now," Will said.

"I wanted everything about your lives to be your choice, not mine," Linc said. "That all of you choose to be involved in the family business is a thrill to me, your mother and your grandfather."

"It sure is," Elmer said. "My parents would be tickled pink to see what you all have done with their modest little store."

"I think we should go to Philly," Ella said, "and, like Hunter said, show them what became of your life with Mom."

"It's four days before Christmas," Charley said.

Thanks to the catalog, they were enjoying the busiest holiday season in the store's history. And sure enough, women from all over had come looking for the "models" who'd made the catalog such a hit. Linc's sons, sons-in-law and nephew had had to keep a low profile lately.

"My sister said my father doesn't have much time," Linc said. "And I don't expect you guys to come. I know how busy this time of year is for all of us—at work and at home."

"I want to go," Charley said. "I wouldn't miss it for anything, but we'll need to figure out some coverage at work if we're all going."

"Let's work on that in the morning," Hunter said. "I'll take care of arranging transport. I've driven to Philly before, so I know it'll be the same amount of time to drive as to fly from Burlington. We'll go after lunch tomorrow, spend one night and come back the day after?"

After the others nodded in agreement, Hunter said, "Great. Plan to be at the store to leave around two."

"I have to bring Caden," Max said.

"You could leave him with Aunt Hannah," Molly said. "If you think the trip will be too much for him."

"I don't want to be away from him that long. So if no one minds, I'll just bring him."

"Of course we don't mind," Linc said.

"I'm going to bring Callie, too," Hannah said. "It's too late for Nolan to plan for a day off at the garage."

"Gavin will want to come, with the baby due in just a couple of weeks," Ella said. "He'll flip his lid if I tell him I'm going away without him."

"Bring him," Linc said. "Anyone who feels the need to come is welcome. Just let Hunter know. And you guys... It means so much to me that you want to come."

"We'd never let you do this without us," Will said.

Each of them hugged him and Molly on their way out, leaving Linc emotionally overwhelmed by the time he and his wife were alone in the family room.

"Well," she said, "aren't they something?"

"They sure are."

"How do you feel after sharing the story with them?"

"Drained after reliving it, but the kids wanting to come really lifted me up. I didn't expect that at all."

"Why not? You raised them to be there for each other. Of course they'd want to be there for you as you take this difficult journey."

"I've never been more proud of them than I was just now. They heard what happened, and all they wanted to know was how they could help."

"We raised them to be independent and to look out for each other and those less fortunate. Loyalty runs deep in this family, and just as they know there's nothing you wouldn't do for them, they feel the same way about you."

"That makes me one lucky dad."

"It's not just luck, Linc. You made sure your kids would never feel the way you did when your father forced you to choose him or the life you wanted. They respect you for that as much as everything else you've done for them."

"I suppose so."

She leaned her head on his shoulder as she continued to hold his hand. "You know what I think we ought to do?"

"What's that?"

"Have an early dinner and then turn in to continue reminiscing about the parts of our story that belong only to us."

"Would this be like a live reenactment?"

Molly laughed, and as always, the sound of her laughter eased the ache inside him. "That could be arranged."

"Sounds like the perfect evening." And, he thought, it was just what he needed after this emotionally charged day.

HUNTER DROVE HOME IN INKY DARKNESS THAT CAME SO EARLY this time of year that it seemed like they got about ten minutes of daylight. It was more than that, of course, but since he worked long hours inside, he didn't get to enjoy it most days. In addition to the darkness, he felt weighted down by the story his father had shared.

With his first child due in late January, Hunter couldn't imagine ever giving that precious child an ultimatum the likes of which his grandfather had given his father. The thought of that kind of horrific choice made him sick, and knowing now what his dad had given up to have a life with Molly made him admire his parents and their marriage even more than he already had.

You just never knew what some people went through to get to where they were always meant to be. Of course, he'd wondered about his father's family, understood there must've been a rift and had questions about it, but because it seemed like a painful topic, he hadn't asked about it. To hear the full story had been shocking, to say the least.

He pulled up to the home he shared with Megan, and the first thing he noticed was that she'd turned on the holiday lights he'd strung on their porch and in the shrubs. The inside lights were on, too, and knowing she was in there, waiting for him to get home, made him happier than anything ever had. If he had her, he had everything he needed, so Hunter completely understood his father's determination to make a life with the woman he'd felt that way about.

The air was crisp and cold, like always this time of year, which had become his favorite time now that he was married to Megan. When it snowed, everything came to a halt for a while—and he got to snuggle in with her and their dog, Horace. He came through the unlocked front door to find her passed out on the sofa in front of the Christmas tree. The lights cast a warm, cozy glow over her pretty face.

In her third trimester, she was tired all the time, but absolutely refused to slow down at the diner. Soon he'd talk to his grandfather, who actually owned the diner, about finding someone to replace her for a few months so she could take time off before and after the baby's arrival.

He would've gotten away with sneaking in if Horace hadn't jumped up from where he was sleeping next to Megan to bark at Hunter.

"Hush," he whispered to the dog. "Mommy's sleeping."

"Not anymore," Megan muttered.

"Sorry. I tried to be quiet, but *someone* wasn't having that."

Horace gave a playful yip.

Hunter kissed the top of the dog's head the way he did every night when he got home. He loved the routines and rituals of having his own family and couldn't wait for their little one to arrive to make what was already perfect that much better. "How're you feeling?" he asked as he sat on the coffee table and leaned in to kiss her.

"Pretty good. Just tired and fat."

"You're not fat. You're pregnant."

"I'm pregnant from head to toe."

"You're adorable." He pushed the blonde hair back from

her face, which was fuller thanks to pregnancy. "Did you get the message I left you?"

"I did. What's up with your parents?"

"You won't believe it."

"They're okay, right?"

"They are, but you know how we never talk about my dad's family?" When she nodded, he said, "It turns out that's because my grandfather forced my dad to choose between my mom and his original family."

"*What?* Seriously?"

Hunter gave her an abridged version of the story his parents had told them.

"Oh my God. That must've been so awful."

"It was, but he said emphatically that he never regretted his choice because he got to spend his life with my mom."

"That's so sweet and romantic."

"Except for the part where he never saw his mother or siblings again."

"I can't even imagine that."

"Neither can I. If anyone had asked me to choose between you and my siblings…"

"It's monstrous. Why did he decide to tell you this now?"

"His father is dying and wants to see him."

"No… No way. He's not going, is he?"

"We're all going. Tomorrow. We'll be gone one night."

"Why, Hunter? Why would he go there after what that man did to him?"

"Because he needs the closure, I think, and maybe he's hoping to reconnect with his siblings."

"What about his mother?"

"She died a few years ago."

"Without ever again seeing her son. What a tragedy for both of them."

"I know."

"Promise me we'll never let anything come between us and our children. No matter what they might choose that we don't agree with..."

"That's an easy promise to make, unless they grow up to be serial killers, of course."

She gasped and then laughed. "Hunter! They're not going to be serial killers!"

"I'm just saying. That's my only line in the sand. Everything else is on the table."

"Good to know."

"Don't worry, honey. I'd never let something like that happen in either my original family or our family. I wouldn't be able to bear it."

"Me either. So you're going away tomorrow, then."

"You want to come? I'm probably going to rent the same bus that took us to Boston last summer. There're too many of us to deal with flying."

"I'd love to go, but I think it'd be too much for me right now. You go, support your dad and hurry home."

"I don't want to leave you here alone."

"I won't be alone, Hunter. I assume not every member of the family will be going. There'll be others around if I need anything."

"You can't need anything when I'm not here to get it for you."

"I'll try my best not to."

He took her hand and brought it to his lips. "You know I'd never leave you for any reason, even for just a night, if I didn't really feel like I had to, right?"

"Of course I know that, and you absolutely have to be there for your dad. I love that you were the one who said let's show them what came of this choice he made."

"I bet his siblings don't know he has ten kids."

"It's unreal, especially in this day and age when people are so connected. Well, everywhere but here in the cell phone wasteland known as Butler, Vermont."

"The Butler disconnect probably saved my dad from having to see and hear all the things his family was doing without him."

"That's true." She held out her arms, inviting him onto the sofa with her.

"Move it, Horace."

The dog whimpered but gave up his space next to Megan.

"The poor guy. I know how he feels. I wouldn't want another guy moving in on my territory either."

"I have plenty of love for both of you."

Hunter kissed her, sighing with the same pleasure he experienced any time she was nearby. "Not sure I can stand even one night away from you."

"It'll be fine."

As he wrapped his arms around her and held on tight to the love of his life, he could only hope that was true.

CHAPTER NINE

"When you've seen beyond yourself, then you may find,
peace of mind is waiting there."
—George Harrison

*H*annah arrived home to a large bull moose standing in her front yard, mooing loudly enough to wake the dead, and a younger moose inside her house, mooing back in anticipation of what she'd taken to calling the daily playdate.

In her car seat, Callie, who'd soon be one, joined in the mooing.

Nolan despaired that his baby girl had mooed before she'd talked.

Hannah was secretly thrilled that her daughter was growing up with the same love for animals that Hannah had. "Take it easy," she said to Fred when she got out of the car.

He came right over to her, nudging her with his cold wet nose. Nolan would lose his mind if he saw Fred that close to his pregnant wife and baby daughter. But what he couldn't seem to understand was that Hannah *knew* down to her soul that Fred would never hurt her. How she knew that, she couldn't explain. She just did. She had such faith in him that she even let him nuzzle Callie, but only when Nolan wasn't around to lose his shit.

Fred was family. They didn't need to worry about him.

From inside, Dexter was making a racket and possibly damaging the new steel door Nolan had installed after Dexter had gotten a little too enthusiastic one day and split the wood door right down the middle.

Naturally, Nolan had taken advantage of that incident to remind Hannah of why moose belonged outside and not inside their home. And she'd reminded him that Dexter was part of their family, and as such, he had every right to split the door if the door could be split to begin with.

Nolan had been unamused, but he'd replaced the door anyway. Hannah was well aware that it wasn't easy to be married to her, but, as she liked to tell him, he knew she was a loon when he married her.

"I had no idea the level of looniness I was signing on for," he'd say every time she reminded him that he'd taken her on "as is."

Hannah opened the door to let Dexter and their dog, Homer Junior, into the yard for their daily playdate with Fred.

Callie squealed with delight as the three friends greeted each other with jubilation that filled Hannah with joy the likes of which she'd once thought she'd never experience again. It had taken many years, as well as Nolan, Callie, Homer Junior, Dexter, Fred and the routine that framed their days, to finally recover as much as she ever would from the devastating loss of her first husband, Caleb, in Iraq.

As she sat on the stairs in the cold December chill, holding her baby girl while the animals frolicked, Hannah was filled with contentment. Today, however, her contentment was tinged with sorrow after hearing her father's story. She'd been curious all her life about his side of the family, about whether she had grandparents, aunts, uncles or cousins. Now that she knew the full tale, she wasn't sure how she felt about people who should've been close family to her and her siblings but were instead strangers.

What they'd done to her dad defied belief.

She held on tighter to Callie, who squirmed to get free and then let out a happy scream as Nolan's truck came into view.

Her daughter was an unrepentant daddy's girl.

When Nolan was out of the car and done scowling at the frolicking moose, Hannah let Callie go to toddle her way to him, her gait reminiscent of a drunken sailor. Hannah had never seen anything more perfect than the way her husband lit up at the sight of his daughter, scooping her up and making her shriek with laughter that had both moose and Homer stopping their game to make sure their little girl was all right.

Seeing Nolan, they resumed their game.

Their little family was unconventional, but Hannah wouldn't have it any other way.

"I see it's the usual circus around here," Nolan said as he leaned in to kiss Hannah. "No Savannah today?"

Hannah normally took care of Dani's daughter during the week. "Dani's parents are here for Christmas and staying at a B&B two towns over. They had her today. We just got home a few minutes before you."

"From where?"

"Family meeting at the barn."

"What's that about?"

"I'll tell you inside. I don't want her out in this cold for too long, and Dex will be looking for his dinner."

"What about my dinner?" Nolan asked with a grin. He cooked as many nights as she did, so he wasn't being sexist.

"We'll see about that, too."

"Is everything okay, Han? You're doing that thing with your eyebrows that happens when you're wound up about something."

Hannah loved that he knew her so well, he could read her moods with a single glance. "Let's go in." She got up to lead the way, with Nolan carrying Callie as he followed her. Knowing it was dinnertime, Dex and Homer were right behind them, leaving Fred alone in the yard to moo his protest over the end of playtime.

"Don't even think about inviting him in here," Nolan said with a scowl.

"You're not allowed to tell me what to think about."

"In this case, I am."

"Just because you're still mad that Dexter outsmarted you doesn't mean you have to take it out on me." She took off Callie's hat and coat and hung them on a hook by the door before removing her daughter's tiny snow boots. Once free, Callie took off running. They laughed at how she'd gone from barely standing to running in a matter of days.

"Are you ever going to let me forget that Dexter outsmarted me?"

"Not in this lifetime." Hannah shot him a saucy smile over her shoulder as she headed for the kitchen to feed her boys. A couple of months ago, after Dex had gotten a little too comfortable with life inside the house, Nolan had told her it was time to let him go before it was too late for him to learn the things he needed to know to survive in the wild.

Hannah had been heartbroken at the thought of Dexter living anywhere but with her, but she'd agreed to let him go —if that was what he wanted. She'd let Dexter out into the yard for the first time without supervision to wait for Fred to come to play. Hannah had stayed in the house and watched from the window, trying not to cry at the thought of Dexter leaving with Fred, who'd tried to lure him away before.

And when he'd sprinted after Fred, her heart had shattered into a million pieces. She'd sobbed so hard, she'd woken Callie from her nap early.

However, hours later, after they'd gone to bed for the night, Dexter had returned, smacking his hooves against the door.

Hannah had bolted out of bed and gone to let him in.

Much to Nolan's dismay, he'd never tried to leave again.

She knew they'd have to figure out a different plan—or buy a bigger house—before Dex was fully grown, but for now, he slept on his oversized dog bed in front of the fire every night, ate from a bowl next to Homer's and was part of their family, even if people (including her own husband) thought she was insane. Maybe she was, but she loved Dex like family and was so thankful he'd chosen to stay with them, even if Nolan groused about it on a daily basis.

"So what happened at the barn?" Nolan asked, holding Callie as he cracked open a beer.

Hannah checked the crockpot of minestrone soup she'd made earlier. "You won't believe it."

By the time she finished telling him the whole story, he'd helped Callie eat her dinner of pasta and vegetables.

"That's seriously messed up," Nolan declared. "What's your dad going to do?"

"He's going there tomorrow, and we're all going with him."

"How come everyone is going?"

"Because we want them to see what came of the choice they forced him to make." Even as she said the words, her heart ached with grief for her dad and what he'd had to give up to be with the woman he loved. The story had touched her deeply as she tried to picture life without the two men she'd loved or being forced to choose between them and her parents and siblings.

The thought of it made her shudder.

And then Nolan was there with his hands on her shoulders and his lips brushing over her hair. "You're upset."

"Hearing what they put him through... It was awful. I always wondered why we didn't see or hear about his family, and now that I know why..."

"You wish you didn't."

"Right. How can I be related to someone who'd do such a thing to his own son?"

"Aww, Han, you're nothing like that. You have a baby moose *living in your house*. I think it's safe to say those genes passed you by."

She laughed through her tears as she turned to face him. "How do you always know just what to say to me?"

"I speak Hannah."

Wrapping her arms around him, she leaned into him, thankful as always for his steady presence. "Thank goodness someone does."

"I'm dirty, sweetheart. Let me go take a shower and change so we can continue this conversation."

Hannah held on tighter, certainly accustomed by now to the scents of motor oil, gas and grease that came home from the garage with him. He told her she was weird because she liked those smells. "Don't go yet."

"I'm here."

They stood there for a long time, until Callie squeaked, wanting to be released from the high chair.

"Are you taking my little girl with you on this trip?"

"I'll have to since you're working and everyone else is going with me. I could ask Aunt Hannah to take her, but I'd hate to be away from her even for a day."

"I'll take the day off if you want to leave her at home."

"You don't have to. I don't mind taking her."

"What am I supposed to do without my ladies tomorrow night?"

"Snuggle Dex?"

"That is *not* happening."

"You will feed him, though, right?"

"Yes, Hannah," he said with a long-suffering sigh. "I'll feed him."

EVER SINCE HIS SON, CHASE, WAS BORN IN JUNE, WILL WANTED to be with him all the time. The chunky blond baby was the center of his parents' lives and had made what was already the best time in Will's life that much better. During Cameron's seemingly endless pregnancy, he'd had to live with the bone-deep fear of something going wrong, the way it had for her mother and grandmother, both of whom had died in childbirth.

He'd even held off on allowing himself to feel anything for his unborn child until he knew for certain that his beloved wife would survive the birth. They'd done everything they could to ensure a safe birth for both mother and baby, but until it actually happened, Will had remained stubbornly unemotional when it came to the baby.

Now that he'd had six months with his son, that detachment seemed like a lifetime ago. He was so in love with the little guy, it wasn't even funny, and more in love with Cam than he'd ever been. Before Chase arrived, he wouldn't have thought it possible to love Cameron more than he already did, but seeing her as a mother, especially knowing she'd grown up without hers, had made his feelings for her that much deeper.

She was a beautiful, devoted, dedicated mother, and their son was lucky to have her.

These days, she worked mostly from home, which meant he missed her during the days they used to spend together. But they agreed that her being with Chase, especially the first year, was for the best.

Which was why his daily goal was to get home as early as possible. Rattled after the family meeting, he tried to process the things he'd learned about his father's family. He drove past the spot where he'd met Cameron on a cold, muddy spring night after she ran into Fred and smashed up her brand-new car. Thinking of that night always made him smile. Even with two black eyes from the airbag, she'd been the loveliest woman he'd ever seen, and he'd been instantly intrigued by her.

Reliving the euphoria of his earliest days with Cameron made him feel sad for what his dad had gone through after meeting his mom. No one should have to make the kind of choice his grandfather had forced his father to make. It was obscene. He gripped the steering wheel tighter as he thought about how awful that must've been for his dad. Linc would say it hadn't been a decision at all. Of course he'd chosen Molly, but the heartbreak of losing everyone else he loved had to have been dreadful.

Will pulled into the long driveway that led to their newly expanded cabin, which was finally finished after a months-long renovation. Living in the midst of construction with a newborn wasn't something he was eager to do again any time soon. But the end result had been worth the chaos. They'd added two big bedrooms, a master bathroom and a much larger family room onto the back of the house, tripling their living space.

With just a few days until Christmas, he loved coming home to the house lit up with the lights he'd strung and smoke curling out of the chimney, while knowing the two people he loved the most were inside waiting for him. When he got out of his truck, their dogs, Trevor and Tanner, appeared out of the darkness to welcome him home.

"What's up, boys?" he asked as they escorted him to the mudroom door through cold air that smelled of snow.

One of them barked, and the other followed suit, both of them running in circles that would've tripped someone who wasn't used to their antics. The dogs were crazy about Chase, who was equally obsessed with them, thank goodness. He stepped into the warmth of home and the scent of the evergreen candles that Cameron burned constantly this time of year.

"Daddy's home," he called out as he removed his boots and hung up his coat.

As he did every night, Chase let out a scream of excitement when he heard Will's voice, making his daddy smile from the thrill of being so loved.

Cameron and Chase were in the new family room, sitting by the huge Christmas tree he'd hauled in, with a fire in the hearth as they played with toys.

Will scooped up his son and spun him around, loving the way the baby's face lit up with pleasure at the sight of him. "How's my big boy?"

"He's great, but don't shake him up, or you might end up wearing his dinner."

Will hugged him close, breathing in the clean smell of him. He'd become addicted to the scent of baby since Chase arrived. He sat on the floor with the baby on his lap and leaned in to kiss his gorgeous wife. Her long blonde hair was piled on top of her head in a bun, and her eyes were tired from a long day of trying to work while taking care of a baby. Her smile, however, was joyful.

"We missed you today," she said.

"I missed you guys like crazy. I need to start working from home more often so you can get a break and I can spend more time with him. There's no reason it has to fall all on you."

"We've already had this 'fight,' remember? You can't breastfeed him."

"No, but I can work from home and help you with him while we're both trying to work. You're tired, baby. You've got dark circles under your eyes."

She reached up to touch them, and he immediately felt like an ass for mentioning them. "I know. I hate them."

"You're the most beautiful girl in the entire world, dark circles or not, but I don't want you getting run-down trying to do it all."

"It's just been really busy with the catalog and the holidays. It'll get better in January."

He put his arm around Cameron and brought her into the snuggle with Chase. "I have to go away for a night."

She looked up at him. "When?"

"Tomorrow."

"How come?"

"That's a long story that I want to tell you after we get him down."

"Is everything okay?"

"Yeah, it is, but one night away is something I've got to do for my dad."

Over the next hour, they worked together to get Chase down for the night and then brought the chicken curry she'd made in the Crock-Pot to sit in front of the fire to eat. Will poured the half glass of chardonnay that she allowed herself while breastfeeding and a full glass for himself.

"What's up with your dad?"

Will told her a condensed version of the story his dad had relayed to them earlier, watching her face go flat with shock and dismay over what had happened so long ago. "And now his dad is dying and apparently wants to see him. We decided to go with him."

"I can't believe he's actually going after what that man did to him."

"I know. Part of me wishes he wouldn't subject himself to the potential hurt of it, but I can understand his need for some sort of closure. If he doesn't go, he might regret it. This way, he's truly the better person."

"I guess. It's just hard to believe his father gave him that kind of ultimatum."

"It's horrible. I feel so bad for him. It must've been heartbreaking to lose his family that way."

"I've always admired your parents, but now I do even more."

"My mom said she was concerned for a very long time that he'd one day resent her for what he'd given up for her. I knew he'd given up going to Oxford for her, but I had no idea the full extent of it."

"I would've felt the same way she did. My God, what an awful thing to do to someone you're supposed to love and protect. It makes me sick."

"Me, too."

"I'm glad you're going with him so his family can see what came of their love."

"That's what Hunter said when he suggested we go."

"The twelve of you will make quite a statement."

"That's the idea, but I'll hate being away from you and Chase for even a night."

"You'll be back before you can miss us."

He shook his head and tipped her chin up to receive his kiss. "I miss you the second I leave you. And I miss you every second that your feet aren't wrapped around mine under the desk at work."

As they kissed again, Will pushed the coffee table away to make room for them to stretch out in front of the fire. He always wanted her, but recalling how tired she was, he slowed the kiss before withdrawing.

"What?" she asked as she ran her fingers through his hair.

"You're so tired."

"Not too tired to kiss my sexy husband."

"Kissing usually leads to other things that you're too tired for."

"I'm not too tired for what kissing leads to."

"Are you sure?"

"Very sure." To make her point, she wrapped her legs around his hips and pressed her heat against his hard cock.

Will laughed at her not-so-subtle message. "Well, all righty, then."

CHAPTER TEN

"There's nothing you can know that isn't known."
—John Lennon

*E*lla was already home and enjoying a cup of
decaffeinated tea when Gavin came in from work,
his face flushed from the cold and his thick dark hair tousled.
He was, without any doubt, the sexiest man she'd ever met,
and some days she still wanted to pinch herself to believe he
was actually hers.

"What's up with your parents?" he asked, his brows
furrowed with worry that reminded her of how he'd often
looked before she made him fall in love with her.

"How do you know something's up?"

"I saw Lucas."

"Where'd you see him?"

"I can't tell you that because it involves Christmas
presents."

Gavin came over where she was seated on the sofa, kissed
her and took a long studying look at her face, as he did every

night to make sure she was all right. She teased him about treating pregnancy as if it were a potentially fatal illness. But after what he'd been through losing his brother and closest friend, she indulged him in whatever he needed to find the peace of mind that had been so elusive for him since Caleb died.

"Luc said there was a family meeting, but I should get the deets from you. So give 'em to me."

She reached for his hand to bring him down to sit with her.

"They're okay, right? I've been in a panic trying to figure out what's wrong. We just saw them, and they were fine."

"I love you so much for the way you love my family."

"Of course I do. They've been part of my life for a long time." His family had moved to Butler when he and Caleb were in middle school. They'd been friends with her brothers from the start, and she'd been in love with Gavin for almost as long as she'd known him. She could barely remember a time when she hadn't been in love with him. That she got to be with him every day now was the greatest blessing in her life.

"My parents are fine, but something happened with my dad's family."

"I don't remember ever hearing much about them."

"Because he never talks about them, and now we know why." She shared the story she'd heard for the first time earlier, still finding it hard to believe even after having had a couple of hours to process it. "We're going there with him tomorrow so he can see his father and show him what's come of the marriage he was so opposed to."

"Wait. You're going where?"

"Philadelphia."

"You can't do that, El. You're nine months pregnant."

"We're not flying. We're taking the same bus we used to

go to Boston. Hunter said it'll be just as long as it would be to fly from Burlington."

"That's like six hours or something."

"Seven. I checked online."

"Ella… Fourteen hours on a bus when you're nine months pregnant? You can't do that. What if you go into labor or something happens or…"

She put her finger over his lips. "I'll be fine. I'm not due for three more weeks."

"Neither was Cameron, but she went weeks early."

"That's very rare with first babies. I don't think we need to worry. It's down and back in two days."

"I don't like it."

"Why don't you come with us so you can be right there if I need you?"

"You wouldn't mind that?"

"I'd rather you come than be wound up in knots the whole time I'm gone."

"Sign me up."

She caressed his handsome face. "Figured you might say that."

"You were all ready for me, weren't you?" he said with a hint of a smile.

"Maybe just a little."

"What did I ever do without you to keep me calm?"

"When are you ever calm?"

"Haha, I'm a lot calmer with you than I was without you, and I'll be back to what counts for normal for me after our baby arrives safely."

She rested her head on his shoulder, knowing for sure he'd worry obsessively about their baby once he or she arrived, but that was okay. She'd be there to keep him sane. "That's good to know. I don't like to see you so spun up."

"I can't help it. You're the most important person in my

life. The thought of you being in any kind of danger makes me crazy."

"I'm not in danger, Gav," she said, laughing. "I'm pregnant."

"Don't act like shit can't go sideways with having a baby, because it can."

"I'm fine. I'm going to *be* fine."

"You can't know that for sure."

"No, I can't, just like we can't know for sure that we'll be okay every time we get into a car or leave the house or walk down the street."

"Great, now I have all that stuff to worry about."

She laughed and elbowed his ribs. "I understand the reason why you worry the way you do, but it makes me ache for you. I want you to find a way to relax and enjoy the life we have together."

"I enjoy every second of our life together, which is why I worry so much about something happening to ruin it. Somehow I survived losing Caleb, but if anything ever happened to you…"

"It's not going to. We just have to believe that everything will be fine. Have faith."

"I'm working on that. It's your fault for making such a mess of me that I can't stand the thought of being without you for even a day or two."

She arched a brow. "How is that my fault?"

"You relentlessly pursued me and made me fall in love with you."

Flashing a satisfied grin, she said, "I was rather relentless, wasn't I?"

"Thank God for that, because I was too stupid to see what was right in front of me, waiting to make me the happiest guy in the world."

"I'm glad you're happy. That's all I've ever wanted for

you."

"I never could've gotten there without you."

"I know! That's what I tried to tell you for so long."

Laughing, he drew her into a soft, sweet, lazy kiss that made her so, so thankful that he'd finally come around to seeing things her way. She'd always known, in her heart of hearts, that they could have something special. The only one who hadn't been convinced was him, until she showed him the error of his ways by loving him as fiercely as she possibly could.

"I was thinking we ought to get married over Christmas," she said. "Just us and the families, no fuss, no big deal."

He leaned his forehead against hers. "When I marry you, my sweet Ella, it'll be the biggest deal of my life."

Smiling, she kissed him again. "Mine, too, but we don't need the fuss of a big production."

"Every girl dreams of the big production."

"Not me. I only ever had one dream when it came to my wedding, and it's already come true because I got the groom I always wanted. So yes to a small wedding at Christmas?"

"Yes to whatever you want. Anything at all."

"I've got everything I've ever wanted already. This'll just make it official."

"I'm all for making it official so you can't get away from me."

"I'm not going anywhere."

CHARLEY WAS AS TENSE AS SHE COULD RECALL BEING IN A VERY long time. Hearing what her poor, sweet dad had gone through with his father… It made her furious. And sad. She banged around the kitchen, getting out pots to make pasta and sauce, her go-to dinner when she hadn't given a thought to what to make until it was time to eat.

Tyler was home all day, working from his office, and made dinner most of the time, but on days he got too busy, it fell to her to make something when she got home. It was a good thing that pasta was one of his favorite things to eat.

She continued to clatter around, taking her frustrations out on the pots and pans until he appeared in the kitchen, his brown hair standing on end, dark-framed glasses making him look sexy and smart, earbuds still in place and a perplexed look on his face.

"I could hear you over my meeting," he said, removing the wireless buds, "and I had the volume turned up."

"Sorry."

"It's okay. We were done. Mostly." He took a closer look at her. "What's wrong?"

"Everything. Every single thing is wrong, and people suck."

"You're just finding that out now?"

"I'm just finding out that people in my own family suck."

He was taken aback by that. "Your family is awesome. Who are you fighting with?"

"It's part of the family you don't know. Hell, I don't know them because they cut my dad out of their lives when he decided to marry my mom and run her family's business rather than theirs."

"*Whoa.* And you just found this out?"

"We all did. He told us the story for the first time today."

Leaning his hip against the counter, he gave her his full attention as usual. No one had ever *seen* her quite the way he did, which had annoyed the shit out of her before he showed her that being seen and loved by him was rather sublime once she stopped fighting it. "What brought this on?"

"His dying father, who's apparently grown a conscience all of a sudden."

"How so?"

"He asked to see him—and he's going. *We're* going. Tomorrow. All of us."

Tyler processed that news in his usual thoughtful way. "That's good. He shouldn't have any regrets."

"What regrets would he have when he was the one *banished* by his own family?"

"Your dad is one of the kindest, most decent people I've ever met. If his father asked him to come and he didn't, he would regret that."

"It's preposterous to me that he's been put in this position after four *decades* of complete silence from them."

"Yes, I can tell you're upset by the clattering."

"It's infuriating!"

Tyler took a step forward and put his arms around her, even though she didn't want him to.

She wanted to continue to rant and rage and clatter the pans, which strangely made her feel better.

"Take it easy, sweetheart. Your blood pressure has to be through the roof."

"I hate mean people, and finding out I'm related to one…"

"I know," he said, rubbing soothing circles on her back that made her want to purr.

How did he do that? How did he take her from the red zone to purring in a matter of seconds? It was his superpower, because no one else in the history of Charley Abbott had ever been able to do what he could. She knew her brothers referred to him, behind her back, as the Charley Tamer, which would piss her off if it weren't so true.

"Not sure how you do that."

"Do what?" he asked.

"Make me forget why I was in a rage ten seconds ago."

His low rumble of laughter made her smile. "All I did was hug you."

"Apparently, that's all it takes to tame me—and yes, I know my brothers call you the Charley Tamer."

"I've never heard that."

She looked up at him. "Don't ruin your very high approval ratings by lying to my face. You do too know about that."

"I can neither confirm nor deny knowledge of said nickname out of fear of losing my magic taming powers."

"It would take a lot for you to lose your powers."

"If I ever do, you'd let me know, right?"

"I think you'd already know. From what I've been told by those closest to me, I'm a bit 'unruly' when I'm not being tamed by you."

"Don't let anyone tell you you're anything other than perfect."

She snorted with laughter. "My siblings have been pointing out my faults since the day I was born."

"That's because they don't get that your faults are part of what make you perfect."

"Said the man who's sleeping with me."

"Mmmm, and I know just *how* perfect you really are," he said, nuzzling her neck right as the water on the stove began to boil.

They broke apart, laughing.

Charley turned down the heat under the pot and looked up at him. "Thanks."

"For what?"

"Whatever it is you do to keep me sane. It's really a gift to me."

He brought her back into his arms, running his hands over her back and down to cup her ass. "You're a gift to me, every delightful inch of you, even when you're in a rage."

Charley closed her eyes and allowed herself to wallow in the comfort only he could provide.

"How long am I going to have to live without you?" he asked.

"Two days and one night."

"That's a really long time. I'd better make sure I inject you with a good dose of my special Charley-Taming Elixir tonight so you're fully declawed before you spend all those hours with your siblings."

She shook with silent laughter. "That's probably a good idea."

UNDER NORMAL CIRCUMSTANCES, YOGA WAS WADE'S ANSWER to anything stressful or upsetting, especially when his wife, Mia, was in Boston visiting her dad. Tonight, yoga wasn't doing it for him. He wished Mia was home so he could vent to her about the many ways his afternoon had been seriously fucked up.

Instead, he went through the motions while his mind raced and his heart ached for his poor dad. No amount of stretching or breathing was going to help him find his Zen tonight. He gave up after half an hour and was coming out of the shower when the house phone rang.

Hoping it was Mia calling, he ran for the extension in the bedroom and picked it up right before the call would've gone to voicemail.

"Why are you out of breath?" his wife asked.

"I was running from the shower to grab the phone."

"Ah, okay. I was hoping you hadn't found a new wife to replace me since I've been away."

"Nah, it took me a long time to find the wife I have. I think I'll keep her for a while longer."

Her laughter made him smile as he yearned for her. He was so far gone over her that spending even one day without her was almost unbearable, and she'd been gone three days already. Because they were so busy at work in the final Christmas rush, he hadn't been able to go with her to celebrate an early holiday with her dad and his family. She'd felt guilty leaving her job at the warehouse when they were so busy, but they'd all wanted her to be with her newfound family for their celebration over the previous weekend.

By the time he got back from Philly, it'd be five days since Wade saw Mia, the longest time they'd spent apart in the year they'd been together. But he knew she needed the time with the dad she'd only recently reconnected with, and he loved the bond she'd formed with Cabot.

"So guess who's been here a couple of times?" she asked.

"Who?"

"Your cousin Izzy."

"Is that right?"

"Yep. My dad isn't saying much on what's going on there, but they've definitely seen each other since the wedding."

"Wow, that's cool. I thought she'd been working in Europe the last few months."

"I guess she had been, but she's back now and was here for dinner last night."

"Very interesting."

"What goes on there?" she asked.

"You won't believe it."

"That sounds worrisome."

"We found out today why my dad doesn't ever talk about his family." Wade told her the story, giving her the highlights —or lowlights, such as they were.

"Oh my goodness, Wade. What's your dad going to do?"

"He's going there. We all are. Tomorrow."

"Wow. How're you feeling about that?"

"Conflicted. On the one hand, I get why my dad needs to go. On the other hand, I want him to tell them all to fuck off after the way they treated him."

"I can see both sides of that. Your dad tries to do the right thing, and in this case, that means going there because his dad asked for him. But a part of him must want to tell them to fuck off, too."

"I'm sure he does, but he won't. That's not who he is."

"And thank goodness for that, right?"

"I suppose so."

"I'm sorry you're upset and I'm not there to hug you."

"Talking to you helps."

"When will you be back from Philly?"

"Day after tomorrow, probably pretty late."

"I'll be there when you get home."

He hated that he wouldn't be there when she got home. "I'm counting the minutes. Are you having fun?"

"Lots of fun, as always. I met more of my dad's friends today at the holiday party he had at his office this afternoon. He seems to have an endless number of friends. And I had lunch with my cousin Caroline. She was asking about Max."

"Was she now?"

"Yep."

"Anything in particular?"

"Just whether he's met anyone new since June. I told her I didn't think so, but I honestly wasn't sure. She seemed disappointed that she doesn't hear more from him."

"Is that something I need to tell him?"

"If you find a way to work it subtly into conversation maybe."

"Subtlety is my middle name, baby."

She laughed. "Sure, it is. None of you Abbotts are known for being subtle."

"I'm the most subtle of the unsubtle Abbotts."

"I'll give you that." She let out a deep sigh. "I miss you."

"I miss you more."

"I don't know if that's possible."

"Trust me, it is."

"Will you call me from Philly and let me know how it goes?"

"Of course." He'd borrow Max's cell phone to call her. "Wouldn't miss a day talking to my favorite person."

"I hope it all goes well for your dad and the rest of you, too, so we can enjoy a fabulous Christmas."

"Christmas will be fabulous no matter what, because it'll be our first one together."

"I can't wait."

"Me either."

"I'll be home and waiting for you to call me tomorrow night."

"Will do, honey. Drive carefully coming home. The roads are slick in the mountains."

"I'll be fine. I hope it all goes well for your dad and family in Philly."

"Thanks. Love you."

"Love you more."

"No way," he said.

"Yes way."

"We'll finish this 'fight' when we see each other."

"I'll look forward to that."

CHAPTER ELEVEN

"I feel the older I get, the more I'm learning to handle life. Being on this quest for a long time, it's all about finding yourself."
—Ringo Starr

*A*s he did whenever he was agitated, Colton went straight to the wood pile when he got back to his home atop Butler Mountain. Lucy would still be working in the cabin they called home. After giving his dogs, Sarah and Elmer, perfunctory pats on the head, he picked up his ax and got to work splitting the never-ending pile of wood they needed to heat the cabin through the winter and boil the sap during sugaring season. He split wood year-round, especially when he needed to work out aggravations, like he did now.

Apparently, he was the only one who didn't agree with the plan for the family to traipse to Philadelphia to appease the dying wishes of a man who didn't deserve one minute of their time, let alone two days of their lives at the worst possible time of year for such a mission.

He'd never met his grandfather or even seen a photo of the man, and yet he was able to picture his head on the log before he brought down his ax to split the log in half. That'd been rather satisfying, so he did it again and again until the imaginary head on a stick was good and dead.

Even though it was freezing, he worked himself into a sweat and had his coat and flannel shirt off by the time Lucy came out to find him stripped down to only a thermal T-shirt in twenty-degree weather.

"What's wrong with you?" she asked him, as she did almost every day.

He glanced at her and saw she had a blanket wrapped around her shoulders. Her whiskey-colored hair was in a ponytail with multiple mechanical pencils sticking out of it. She was fucking adorable. "The usual stuff."

"Why're you working like that when you're usually done by now?"

"Because."

"Well, that answers all my questions." She watched him for another minute. "Did something happen?"

"Yes, something happened. I found out my grandfather is a scum-sucking, piece-of-shit asshole."

She gasped.

He looked up to find her sweet face gone blank with shock. "Not Elmer."

"Thank goodness you didn't mean him."

"I mean the other one, the one I've never met. The one who kicked my dad out of his family because he wanted to marry my mom rather than work for the family business and *now...*" He brought the ax down on the imaginary head that apparently wasn't dead enough yet.

Lucy approached him and gently took the ax out of his hand, tossing it aside.

Colton put his hands on his hips, breathing hard from exertion.

"Now what?"

"Now he expects my dad to drop everything and come running just because he's dying and has apparently developed a guilty conscience that he wants to purge before he croaks. And it's all just so *fucked up*."

"Oh, Colton. That's *so* fucked up."

"I'm glad you think so, because everyone else is telling him he should go and take us with him so they can see what came of this marriage they were so opposed to. But I'm like, *whoa*, people. Why in the world would we let him do that when this guy hurt him so badly? It makes no sense to me."

"Let's go inside and talk about it."

"I'd rather stay out here and smash things."

"Is that helping?"

"No, but…"

She took hold of his hand and gave a gentle tug, stopping to scoop up his coat and shirt on the way to the house.

The dogs followed them in and snuggled up together in front of the fire in the woodstove.

"You want a drink?" Lucy asked.

"Yeah, I do. A really big, stiff drink would be good."

"Coming right up."

She poured bourbon straight into a glass and handed it to him.

He drank half of it in one swallow, relishing the burn as it traveled through his system.

"Better?" she asked, watching him warily.

He couldn't have her wary around him. "Much better, baby. Thank you. How are you? How's my little bruiser?"

"We're fine, just worried about you."

"Sorry. Didn't mean to come home hot."

"Where else should you go when you're upset?"

"My dad… He's like the best guy ever, you know?"

"I do know. I absolutely know that, and he raised seven

amazing sons who are just like him in all the ways that matter most."

Colton was appalled to feel a lump form in his throat as tears burned his eyes. He placed his hands flat on the counter and dropped his head. "The thought of someone hurting him that way, especially his own father... It just makes me a little crazy. I was pretending to smash the head of a man I've never met on the logs."

Lucy laughed as she came to him and wrapped her arms around him, compelling him to lean on her, which he did. Happily. She was his favorite person.

"What you said about your dad being the best guy in the world..."

"What about it?"

"That's why he has to go to see his father. You know that, right? Deep inside, despite all the hurt, he's still the dutiful son who goes when his father calls. He wouldn't be able to live with himself if he didn't."

Colton sighed and sagged into her warm embrace. "How do you do that?"

"Do what?"

"Make it seem so logical when it's anything but to me?"

"You're running on emotion. That makes it hard to see the logic."

He wrapped his arms around her and held on tight to her, his love, his rock, his everything. "Thankfully, I've got you to tell me what I should be thinking rather than letting the emotions take over."

"I'm always happy to set you straight."

When he'd arrived home, he would've thought it impossible that he'd laugh at anything tonight, but he laughed at that. Pulling back from her, he looked down at her adorable face and kissed her forehead, the tip of her nose and then her lips, lingering over the sweet taste of her. "Thanks."

"Any time. So does this mean you're going to Philadelphia?"

"I guess it does," he said, sighing.

WORKING THE NIGHT SHIFT AT THE FIREHOUSE AFTER THE FAMILY meeting had Lucas out of sorts, wishing he was able to spend the evening at home with Dani and Savvy and Dani's parents, rather than having to stay at work. He and Landon had to do some juggling to cover their upcoming fire department shifts as well as the final days of sales at the Christmas tree farm that Landon managed so they could go on the trip to Philadelphia.

Before his shift, Lucas had put a rush on finishing the rocking chair he'd made for Ella at Gavin's request. Now that the juggling was done, Lucas was left with a long night to think about everything he'd learned about his family that day.

He wanted Dani, and he needed to tuck in his little girl.

Without worrying about coming up with an excuse for the other guys on duty, he grabbed a radio off the charger and told one of the others he was running home for a minute but would be back. By now, his future in-laws would be settled at the B&B where they were staying, and he could hopefully have a minute alone with Dani.

"Got it, LT," his colleague said without looking up from the book he was reading in the lounge.

They joked that being a firefighter was either deadly boring or the biggest adrenaline rush you could ever experience, with not much in between those two extremes. Thankfully, in Butler, Vermont, it was mostly boring. As he drove the short distance to home, he recalled how he used to yearn for a little more action. Until the Admiral Butler Inn burned to the ground in May and nearly took him—and Landon's now-fiancée, Amanda—with it.

Since then, he had a new appreciation for the boring, the mundane, the routine aspects of life and was just fine with a shift in which they never received a single call. Something about thinking you're going to die before you ever really got the chance to live did something to a guy's sense of adventure. He still loved doing the outdoor exploits he and his brothers were known for, but now that he had a fiancée and daughter to think about, he took his safety much more seriously than he used to. That was especially true knowing how Dani had lost the baby's father in a tragic accident when she was pregnant with Savvy.

Since he met Dani and Savvy and fell in love with both of them, Lucas had *everything* to live for. At home, he ran up the two flights of stairs to their cozy third-floor apartment and used his key in the door he insisted she keep locked when he wasn't home, even though the crime rate in Butler was extremely low. He slept better at the firehouse when he knew they were locked in.

Savvy let out a scream when she saw him and came toddling over to him on unsteady legs. She'd started walking right before her first birthday in November and, like his niece Callie, had advanced quickly to running. The Christmas tree in the corner was decorated only above where she could reach, which was one of many things about her that delighted him.

Lucas scooped her up and gave her a squeeze.

"Lu, Lu, Lu."

"Hi, baby." One of his favorite things ever was the way she recoiled in horror from his identical twin brother. Nothing amused him more than the way she reacted to Landon as she tried to figure out how it was possible that someone else looked almost exactly like her beloved Lu. He kissed her ticklish neck until she screamed with laughter.

"If you rile her up, you own her," Dani said from her perch on the sofa, where she was folding a load of laundry.

He was forever telling her to just stop, take a break and breathe, everything would get done. She was constantly doing something unless he managed to distract her, which he was very good at doing.

Sitting next to her on the sofa, he put Savvy down to toddle about and play with her toys for a few more minutes before bedtime and leaned in to kiss his love.

"Thought you weren't coming home tonight."

"I wasn't going to, but I needed a Dani-and-Savvy fix."

"We're always happy to see you. You know that."

"Did you have a nice dinner with your folks?"

"We did. It's so great having them here."

"Maybe by next year we'll have a place big enough for them to stay with us."

"Maybe." She took a closer look at him. "Is everything okay?"

"Yeah," he said. "Except one thing."

"What's that?"

While she continued to fold clothes, he told her the story his dad had shared earlier. By the time he was finished, she'd stopped folding and was staring at him. "What's he going to do?"

"He's going to Philly tomorrow to see him, and we're all going with him."

"Good," she said, nodding. "You guys should go. He'll need you there with him."

"That was Hunter's thought, and everyone agreed."

"You agree, don't you?"

"I do. Of course I do, but I hate that I have to go without you and my little girl."

"We'll be fine. Go support your dad and hurry home to us. We'll be waiting for you."

"I'm counting on that, baby."

AFTER A LATE-AFTERNOON SHIFT AT THE TREE FARM THAT HAD brought in only a few last-minute stragglers, Landon arrived home to a dark house and tried to remember what Amanda and Stella had planned for the afternoon. He was greeted by Matilda, the yellow Lab puppy Dude had given Stella when she moved in with them, and let the puppy out in the yard, keeping an eye on her as she did her business and then came bounding back in for dinner.

She bounced with happiness at the sight of her full bowl and dove in, making a huge mess, like she did every time she ate. Thankfully, she also cleaned up after herself.

He went to the dry-erase calendar Amanda kept on the wall of the kitchen to see where his girls were. Dance class in St. Johnsbury at five p.m. They should be back soon, he thought, even as he tried not to think about them driving the dark, winding, icy roads between here and there.

Those roads gave him nightmares because he'd seen—far too often—what happened when cars lost control on the curves, especially at this time of year. He'd insisted Amanda get an SUV with four-wheel drive and antilock brakes so she'd be as prepared as possible for driving in Vermont winters.

When you had everything you've ever wanted, the thought of losing it—or them—was unbearable. Six months ago, he'd been single and unencumbered. Now he had a fiancée, a stepdaughter he loved like his own child and a dog who'd quickly worked her way straight into his heart. Life was good, and he was so incredibly grateful for everything he had now.

Maybe that was why his father's story had touched him so deeply. Hearing what his dad had gone through to be with his mom pained Landon. If he'd had to choose between Amanda and his family... The thought of that was unimaginable. Anyone who would force their own child to make that kind of choice had to be a freaking monster.

And that monster was Landon's grandfather.

Great.

He opened a beer and had downed half of it by the time the wash of headlights over the yard reflected inside the house. Excited to see his girls after the long day apart, he went to the door to wait for them. Only Amanda emerged from the car, smiling when she saw him there.

That smile lit up his world and made everything that was wrong seem trivial compared to the many things that were so, so right.

"Where's our girl?"

She pulled a knitted hat off her head, leaving her dark hair charged with static. "She went to have pizza with Emma, Grayson and Simone after dance class. They're bringing her home."

Matilda let out a loud whine when she saw that Stella wasn't with Amanda.

Amanda petted the dog and kissed her head. "She'll be home soon, silly girl. You'll survive another hour without her."

"She's not sure she will," Landon said. "You didn't want to go with them?"

"I figured you'd be home by now, so I came to see you."

He kissed her and hugged her. "I'm glad you did. How was your day?"

"*Crazy* busy." She'd been helping Dani at the warehouse, contending with the rush of last-minute holiday orders. "Your dad is going to be very happy with the company's bottom line this month. The catalog has been a massive success, as we knew it would be."

"People in town are talking about the influx of visitors. Business is booming for everyone, apparently."

She put her hands on his hips and went up on tiptoes to kiss him. "It's due to the hot dudes in the catalog. They're coming to feast their eyes."

He straightened her hair. "Whatever."

Laughing, she drew him into another kiss. "What's wrong?"

"Nothing. I'm kissing my best girl. What could be wrong?"

"Don't lie to me, Landon. I know you, and I can tell when you're upset. I saw it the second I came up the stairs to the porch."

"I can't get anything by you, can I?" he asked, smiling.

"Nope, so don't even try it." She took him by the hand and towed him along with her until they were seated on the sofa, facing each other. "Start talking."

"You know it turns me on when you get bossy with me."

"Everything turns you on."

"Only you." Because he loved her hair so much and took any excuse to play with it, he tucked a strand behind her ear. "I found out today why we never see or hear anything about my dad's family." Over the next few minutes, he told her the story of what had happened when his dad brought his mom home to Philadelphia to meet his family.

"Dear God," Amanda said. "That's horrific."

"I know."

"What brought this on today?"

"My grandfather—and I use that word very loosely—is dying and has asked my dad to come there to see him."

"No way. He's not going, is he?"

Landon nodded. "We all are. Tomorrow."

"Why?"

"Because my dad would regret it if he didn't. He doesn't have to forgive him, but he needs to go so he doesn't have to feel guilty for the rest of his life that he didn't."

"I guess I can see that, but it's outrageous that he'd have the gall to summon your dad there after decades of estrangement."

"Agreed." He linked his fingers with hers. "So, I have to go away for a night tomorrow."

"Aren't you working at barn tomorrow night?"

"Luc and I arranged coverage there and the farm for the next two days so we can go on the trip."

"Ah, okay."

"You understand why we're doing this, don't you?"

"Of course, but I just hate that you have to deal with something like this, that your dad has to deal with it, especially at Christmas."

"I know. It sucked to see him so emotional over what happened all those years ago."

"I'm sure. He's such an upbeat, positive, happy person."

"He is, and to know what he had to give up to have the life he wanted… I just can't stand that for him."

"I don't know him as well as you do, of course, but from what I can see, he's been completely content in the life he's led with your mom and all of you. He loves his family, his work, his community. I wouldn't pretend to speak for him, but from what I've witnessed, he has no doubt he made the right decision."

"He said as much. But still… It had to be so painful to lose touch with his siblings. I wouldn't be able to deal with that."

"The good news is you'll never have to. That won't happen in your family. You guys are so tight. You'd fight for each other no matter what."

"I'd like to think so."

"You would. For sure."

"I bet my dad thought that about his own siblings, too. How'd they let that happen? Their father couldn't stop them from talking to each other."

"Think about the times, Landon. None of the technology we take for granted now. They probably didn't even know what part of Vermont he'd landed in."

"If that'd happened to one of my siblings, I'd have gotten in a car and driven to Vermont and tracked down him or her."

"Unless your father was holding something over you, like money or a job or being banished like your brother was."

"None of that would've stopped me from looking for them."

"Just playing devil's advocate here, but it's easy to say that without knowing the whole story."

"I guess. It's just hard to picture life without even one of my siblings, let alone all of them. That must've been so awful for him."

"I'm sure it was, but I'm also sure the beautiful family he created with your mom helped to fill some of the void." She brought his head to lean on her shoulder and ran her fingers through his hair.

He wallowed in the pleasure of her touch and the way she managed to calm and soothe him. "Thanks for listening."

"Always happy to listen to you."

"Will you girls be okay here by yourself tomorrow night? You could stay with Emma and Gray if you don't want to be here alone." Amanda and Stella had become very close with Emma and Simone over the last few months.

"We'll be fine. We've got Matilda to keep us safe."

He snorted out a laugh. "As long as a potential robber doesn't offer her a piece of steak, she's got you covered."

Hearing the word *steak*, Matilda lifted her head to look at him.

"Stand down, girl," Landon said. "No steak tonight."

Sighing, she dropped her head onto her paws, looking dejected.

"Poor baby. First, I came home without Stella, and then you said the word S-T-E-A-K and didn't deliver. This evening isn't going well for her."

"She'll be okay."

"Will you?"

"I'm much better after talking it out with you. At times like this, I wonder what I ever did before I had you."

"I have a hard time remembering what life was like before I lived in this gorgeous house with you, Stella and Matilda. It's the most perfect life I could ever picture for myself."

"If you're happy, I'm happy," he said, as he often did.

"Same goes, my love. Same goes."

CHAPTER TWELVE

"I get by with a little help from my friends."
—Ringo Starr

*A*s he did every night after dinner and bath time, Max rocked his baby son until he fell asleep, well aware that soon his little boy would be too big to be rocked. Max was determined to stick with their bedtime routine for as long as he possibly could. He'd read an article on one of the parenting sites he followed about how there's a "last time" for everything—the last time you'll ever change their diaper or pick them up or rock them to sleep. Often, you won't know it's the last time until much later when you realize you haven't done those things in a while or they stopped happening without you noticing.

He wasn't ready for any of it to end and could barely believe Caden was already thirteen months old, walking and saying a few words, such as Max's favorite word—Dada. Being Caden's Dada was the best thing to ever happen to Max, even if it was also the hardest thing he'd ever done. While making sure his son had everything he needed, he grappled with the nonstop parental guilt he'd learned was normal, even if it sucked. Did he spend enough time with his son? Was it right to ask his mother to watch him while he was working? Would he be better off in daycare with other kids his age?

Max tortured himself with those and a million other questions, thus his reliance on the parenting sites that were a wealth of information, as were his parents, who'd been there, done that, ten times over. Even though they hadn't been single parents, they'd seen it all with him and his nine siblings and generally knew what he should do in any situation.

"I know you couldn't understand the stuff your Gramps was saying today, buddy," he said softly to Caden, who was on his way to sleep. "But you should know that I'd *never* make you choose between me and the one you love. I'd never, ever do that to you. All I want is for you to do whatever it takes to be happy. I want you to love and be loved and to find your place in this world, whether it's here or somewhere far away. Although, I sure hope you end up close by, because I'd miss you something awful if you weren't around every day. Didn't my grandfather miss my dad after he kicked him out of the family? I hope he regretted what he did. I hope he regretted it every day."

He continued to rock until Caden's little body went slack, but he didn't move to transfer him to the crib. Not yet. Tonight, he needed a little something extra from his son. He needed the comfort of knowing, no matter what happened, that he would love and support Caden in everything he did, even if he didn't necessarily agree with his choices. As long as he was living a healthy, productive life, Max would have his back. It was really that simple.

While holding his son a little tighter, Max rubbed his tiny back and ran his lips over the soft silk of his blond hair. The two of them were a team and always would be, come what may.

From across the hall, he could hear his mother laughing, which happened a lot when his parents were together. They were #couplegoals to Max and his siblings, all of whom had found their perfect match. He hoped his was out there some-where, waiting for him to find her. A year after his relation-ship with Caden's mother had imploded, he was starting to feel ready to take a chance on something new. He'd hoped he'd hear more from Caroline, his sister-in-law Mia's cousin, whom he'd met at Mia and Wade's wedding in Boston and had one great night with. But after a few weeks of regular texts, they'd dropped off to once in a while as they both went on with their lives.

He'd really liked Caroline a lot and had enjoyed the night they'd spent together, but she lived in Boston. He was hours away in Vermont. Unless she relocated to Vermont, she wasn't going to be the solution to his predicament.

After the holidays, he needed to get serious about dating again. As much as he loved being with his parents and appre-ciated their help, he didn't want to live at home forever. He wanted his own home and family and was determined to make that happen. Somehow.

In the meantime, he'd do whatever he could to support his dad through the next few days the way Linc had supported him every minute of his life. That was how fami-lies were supposed to work, and Max couldn't wait for his "grandfather" to see what a great father his son had turned out to be, no thanks to him.

Success was the best revenge, his other grandfather, Elmer, had reminded them earlier, and Linc had been a smashing success as a husband, father, grandfather and busi-nessman.

Max and his siblings would do whatever it took to make sure Linc's father saw that.

Elmer poured himself a glass of Bailey's, tossed another log on the fire and sat to enjoy the snap, crackle and pop of fire that cast a warm, cozy glow over his small home. In the corner stood the Christmas tree that Landon had brought from the farm, as he did every year.

Landon put the lights on for him, and then Ella and Charley decorated it with the ornaments he and Sarah had collected over a lifetime together. Some were from her family, some from his and a great many of them were theirs, made by their kids in school or purchased as mementos from trips or events that make up a life.

His grandchildren took good care of him, always doting on him and making sure he had what he needed. If it were up to him, he wouldn't have bothered with a Christmas tree since he lost his Sarah. But the kids had insisted he needed it, and because he had a long track record of giving his eighteen grandchildren whatever they wanted, he'd ceded to their wishes. They were good kids, every one of them, and he couldn't be prouder of them.

His sons, both quite a bit older than Molly and Hannah, had never married or had kids, and had moved out of state years ago to pursue careers in public safety. His older daughter was married but didn't have children. He was thankful his youngest girls had stayed in Butler to raise their families, which had kept Elmer involved in the daily lives of his grandchildren as they grew up.

The events of the day had brought back so many memories, including the day Molly had stepped off the bus from Mississippi, holding hands with the good-looking young man from Philadelphia, and introduced him as her *boyfriend*. Elmer chuckled to himself at the visceral reaction he'd had to Linc's arrival in Butler—and how wrong he'd been about his future son-in-law.

He'd never told anyone how wrong he'd been, but Sarah had known, because she was the one who'd told him he had it all wrong. Elmer had liked Mike Coleman, the man Hannah had married, from the get-go, but he'd been suspicious of Linc Abbott. He certainly understood what Linc saw in his beautiful Molly, but what did a guy with a Yale MBA and a fancy Philadelphia pedigree want with tiny Butler, Vermont, and Elmer's small-town family business?

Elmer had been hard on the guy for months, waiting for him to show his true colors, but all he'd seen was a genuine young man on fire with ambition and a desire to contribute to the business. And, he'd had to grudgingly admit, he saw how much Lincoln loved Molly.

Then the kids had gone to Philadelphia, where Linc's father dropped the hammer on him. Elmer would never forget the two of them returning to Butler, looking like survivors of a natural disaster.

They'd arrived at dinnertime, and Elmer had seen from the first second they walked in the door that something was terribly wrong. For one thing, they'd lost the sparkle they both had when they were together. For another, they were unusually quiet. It'd taken an hour or maybe two to get the story out of them, and afterward, the four of them had sat in shocked silence so loud it had roared in Elmer's ears.

To this day, he still had no idea how a man could do such a thing to his own child. He'd been a bit extreme in his protectiveness of his precious daughters, but never once had he forced them to choose between him and something or someone else they wanted.

"Daddy," Molly had said that night, taking him aside in

the kitchen while Linc was in the living room with Sarah. "I want you to do something for me. It's something big and important and probably not something you particularly want to do, but it's something I need."

"Anything, sweetheart." At that moment, he would've given anything to see her smile again.

"I need you to marry us. Right now. Tonight. I want Linc to know he has a new family, me and you and Mama and Hannah and Mike and the children we're going to have. We're his family now, and we'll never turn our backs on him."

She was so fiercely beautiful in her outrage and in her love for Linc. "You need a license, sweetheart."

"We'll take care of that tomorrow. Please, Daddy. I know you're still not sure about Linc, but I love him so much, and…" Her eyes filled with tears. "Please."

He was powerless to deny her this or anything she wanted, especially when she'd been so deeply hurt by people he'd never meet or know. "Of course, love. It'd be an honor, and I like Linc. I don't want you to think I don't."

"But you're not sure he's right for me."

"No, I'm sure he's right for you. I'm just not sure he's right for Butler and the life he's decided he wants here."

"He loves it here."

"He loves being here with you. Anyone can see that. I'm concerned about him suddenly getting itchy and deciding a few years down the road that small-town life isn't for him." As soon as he said the words, he regretted them, because the last thing his Molly needed was anyone else raining on their parade.

Molly raised her chin defiantly. "That's not going to happen. He said this is what he wants, that *I'm* what he wants, and after the way his family hurt him, I just want him to know that he has a home here with me and with us. I think he needs that."

"I think so, too, sweetheart."

"You do? Really?"

Elmer swallowed the lump in his throat and nodded. His baby was getting married. Right now, apparently.

"You'll marry us?"

"I will."

"And when we leave here to spend the night at our home, you won't come looking for Linc with the rifle?"

"I'll do my best to resist that temptation."

She flung herself at him, wrapping her arms around him and hugging him as tightly as she had in years. "Thank you so much for being the best dad in the whole world. After what I saw at Linc's house today, I appreciate you even more than I already did."

Touched by the compliment and the emotion behind it, Elmer had hugged her back, even though his heart was breaking at the thought of his sweet girl getting married and leaving home for good. He knew it was the natural order of things, and she was more than old enough, at nearly twenty-three, but he would miss having her sleeping under his roof and eating dinner at his table every night. "Love you, my sweet girl, and I hope you and your Linc will be happy together forever."

"We will, Daddy. I'm sure of it."

Elmer could only hope she was right as she took his hand and towed him into the living room to present her plan to her fiancé.

"Daddy is going to marry us! Tonight."

Sarah looked at Elmer, her brow raised and a thousand questions in her expression.

"What?" Linc said. "We have a wedding planned... January..."

"We'll still have that day, but I don't want to wait any longer for us to be married. Earlier today, you were given an impossible choice, and you chose me. Well, I want you to know that I choose you, too. I choose you for the rest of my life." She got down on her knees in front of him. "Will you marry me tonight, Linc?"

He raised his hands to her face, his eyes shining with unshed tears.

Elmer found himself holding his breath, waiting for him to say something.

"I'd love to marry you tonight, sweetheart."

She let out a happy squeal and kissed him long enough that Elmer was forced to clear his throat to remind the love-birds that they weren't alone.

They broke apart, laughing and teary-eyed and smiling so big he wondered whether a face could actually crack under all that happiness. He was so damned grateful to see them smiling again that he was almost able to forget Linc's impertinence.

"So how does a last-minute wedding without a license work around here?" Linc asked.

"Dad is a justice of the peace. He'll marry us tonight, and we'll take care of getting the actual license tomorrow. It's a little backwards, but it'll be okay."

"As long as I have you, everything is okay," Linc said, kissing the top of her head.

Now that the two of them were about to tie the knot, Elmer was realizing he'd be in for a whole lot more PDA than he'd had to tolerate up until now. *Ugh*, he thought. *I'm so not ready for that.*

"Where do you want us, Dad?"

"How about in front of the fireplace?" Sarah suggested.

"That'd be perfect," Molly said.

He thought she'd want to get changed or put on makeup

or do her hair, but all she wanted, it seemed, was to marry Lincoln Abbott.

Elmer stood before them, gazing down at one of the faces that had ruled his world since she and her siblings were born, and told himself he could do this. He could give her away to another man and entrust her health, safety and happiness to him. Taking a deep breath, he let it out slowly and walked them through the exchange of vows, which were said with tears and laughter and love.

He couldn't deny the presence of love as much as he might've wanted to when she first brought Linc home. They didn't have rings yet, so he skipped that part. "By the power vested in me by the state of Vermont, I now declare you husband and wife. Linc, you may kiss your bride. Chastely."

They laughed as they came together for a kiss that was the furthest thing from chaste.

Elmer looked away, catching the gaze of his own beloved, who wiped away tears. Their darling Molly was a married woman. He stepped away from the newlyweds and went to his own bride, putting his arms around her.

"You did good up there, pal," Sarah said.

"I was trying not to lose it the whole time."

"I know."

"It was the right thing to do this for them, wasn't it?"

"Absolutely. They're going to make a go of it. I'm sure of it."

"Our little girls have ended up with good guys."

"One of them has. The jury's still out on the other one."

Elmer drew back from the hug to look down at her. "What do you mean?"

"I feel pretty confident that Linc will stick. I'm not so sure about Mike."

"Huh. Well, you've never said that before. Did he do something?"

"Not at all. Just a feeling I have, but we don't need to dwell on that tonight when there're happy things to celebrate. Let's find some champagne to toast the newlyweds."

As always, his Sarah had been right about Mike Coleman, who left Hannah with eight children, the oldest of whom had been sixteen at the time, and never looked back. Recalling that dark time in their lives never failed to make Elmer as angry as he'd ever been. Luckily, the Colemans had had him and Linc, and they'd tried to fill the void Mike had left as best they could, but nothing had ever been the same for them after their father left. Or for his daughter Hannah, who'd only recently found new love with Ray Mulvaney after many years alone.

Elmer had found that life was a strange and often wonderful journey that also included its share of heartaches. Losing his Sarah had been the biggest heartache of Elmer's life, followed by the crushing disappointment of his son-in-law leaving his wife and eight children.

But there'd been far more magic than pain in his blessed life, and with the benefit of age, wisdom, perspective and forty years, he counted Lincoln Abbott among the greatest of his many blessings. There was nowhere else he'd rather be than with his son-in-law in Philadelphia to make sure Linc's father knew that Elmer had stepped up to fill the void left by his father's unimaginable actions—and that Elmer loved Linc like a son.

CHAPTER THIRTEEN

*"Love is a promise, love is a souvenir, once given
never forgotten, never let it disappear."*
—John Lennon

*L*inc hadn't expected to laugh after the day he'd had,
but as always, Molly came through for him, teasing
and joking with him until he'd almost forgotten the
pending mission to Philly.

Almost.

"Remember that night we came home from Philadelphia
and what happened next?" she asked.

"How could I ever forget our first wedding?"

They'd never told anyone else that they'd gotten married
that night. Even Molly's sister, Hannah, hadn't known about
it. Only Molly's parents had known, and they'd kept the
secret in the months between that night and their January
wedding.

Linc turned on his side in bed to face her, noting she'd freed
her long hair from the braid she wore it in most of the time.
Her hair was silvery gray now, but still as pretty as it'd been

when they first met. "You had no idea what it meant to me that night to have you ask me to marry you right then and there, or how much I needed it after what'd happened earlier that day."

"I knew what you needed, and that's why I did it. You'd been set adrift, and I wanted to bring you home."

He placed his hand on her face and caressed her soft skin. "*You* are my home. You have been since the day we met, and you always will be."

"Same for me with you. Remember what happened after my dad married us?"

"Is that a trick question? Of course I remember. I remember every minute of that day like it was yesterday."

"Tell me about it. It's my favorite bedtime story."

He drew her in closer to him, his arms around her, her head on his chest, and let his mind wander back in time to the first night they spent together.

Lincoln couldn't believe what Molly had done for him —and for them—by asking her dad to marry them, even if it wasn't yet entirely legal without the license they'd get the next day. It was enough for him, and apparently her parents, who stood at their front door and waved them off as they left in Molly's car to go home to their barn.

"You actually heard him say he wouldn't come after us with the rifle?" Linc asked as he drove them through town on roads that had become familiar to him over the last couple of months, during which Butler had begun to feel like home.

"He promised," Molly said with a lighthearted laugh that made him smile.

"I appreciate you thinking of that detail ahead of time."

"I wanted to change your memories of this day, to give

you something else to think about other than what happened earlier."

"You certainly succeeded. I'll never forget what you did for me today, Mol. Not for the rest of my life."

"I did it for both of us." She looked over at him, flashing the saucy grin he loved so much. "Selfishly, I couldn't wait until January for us to be married or to be able to sleep together every night."

"Mmm, that's the best part of being married, or so I'm told."

"I guess we'll find out."

"Starting tonight." Despite the trauma he'd endured at the hands of his father earlier, Molly had made it so that incident wasn't the headline of their day. She'd stepped up to give him exactly what he hadn't known he needed, and now they had the freedom to be together all the time. Nothing had ever made him happier—or more certain that he'd done the right thing when confronted with his father's ultimatum—than that did.

Linc drove them over the one-lane covered bridge, took a right turn onto Hells Peak Road and pulled into their driveway a few minutes later. "Home sweet home," he said of their ramshackle barn that would someday be a showplace his wife would be proud of. He was determined to give her everything, including a home unlike any other where they could raise a family and make a life.

October was chilly in the mountains, and they didn't yet have heat in the barn. That was the next thing on their endless to-do list to make the barn habitable for the winter. "What do you think of a campfire at the tent?" he asked.

"I think that sounds perfect."

"It's going to be cold out there tonight, Mol."

"No, it won't."

"They said on the radio it's supposed to get down to the low forties."

"We won't be cold."

The certainty in her words sent a shiver of anticipation down his back. They used the bathroom inside and headed out to their backyard campground, where Linc built a fire he hoped would help keep them warm during the night.

Molly had acquired extra blankets somewhere and had brought them with her to add to their bed.

"My wife is always thinking ahead, isn't she?" Linc asked, loving the way the word *wife* sounded.

"She does her best to take good care of her husband."

"She's the best wife he's ever had."

As always, her laughter lit up her face and sent another shiver of delight through him. Knowing he had the rest of his life to spend with her, that he had her to lean on when the going got tough, made the rest of what had happened that day worth it, or so he told himself. He wasn't under any illusions that the days to come would be all sunshine and roses, or that the breach with his family wouldn't hurt forever. But having her to help him through the loss would make it bearable. At least he'd still get to see his siblings. He'd make sure of that.

"Where's my husband?" Molly asked from inside the tent.

"Right here."

"Your wife is lonely."

"We can't have that." He tossed two more logs on the fire and went to find his wife, nearly swallowing his tongue when he saw she was already in bed, under the quilts, her hair loose around her bare shoulders as she held herself up on one elbow.

"What's going on under there?" he asked, tipping his head for a better look at his beautiful wife.

"Come find out."

"Don't mind if I do."

"Just in case you didn't get the invitation, the dress code for this party is naked."

Linc was definitely going to swallow his tongue before she was finished with him. "Good to know." He pulled and tugged at clothes and buttons and zippers with gleeful haste that had his beloved laughing her ass off.

"Quit laughing at me."

"Quit being funny."

He couldn't believe this was actually happening, that after months of longing, he was finally going to be naked in a bed with Molly Stillman. That was when it occurred to him that she was Molly Abbott now, his precious wife, the love of his life, and this was one of the most important moments he'd ever have with anyone. They'd come close the other night, but had held off, mostly because he felt she was still upset after telling him about Andrew. Tonight, he had to make it as perfect for her as she was for him, and he had to keep in mind that this act was tied to grief for her.

Hopefully, that wouldn't always be the case, but her loss of Andrew was part of the equation tonight.

The cold air had him scooting quickly under the covers, where he encountered her warm, naked body. Groaning from the pleasure of her skin against his, he pulled her into his embrace. "This has to be what heaven feels like."

"Mmm," she said. "For sure."

They fell into a deep, sensual kiss that had him dying for more, for everything, in a matter of seconds until he recalled that he'd given no thought at all to birth control since he hadn't known this was going to happen tonight. "Uh, Mol?" He eased back from the best kiss he'd ever had, even with her.

"Yes?"

"We forgot something."

143

"What?"

"Birth control."

"We're all set. I saw my doctor a month ago and got on the pill."

"You... A month ago. Oh."

"I had a feeling we might not make it until January, and correct me if I'm wrong, but we're not exactly ready to have a baby."

"You're not wrong."

"We don't have a stall for him or her yet."

"Very funny, and just so you know, our children will *not* sleep in stalls." He kissed her again, with even more desire than he'd had a minute ago, before he'd known she was protected.

"Whoa," she said, breathless after a kiss that went on for what seemed like hours. "I need to go on the pill more often."

"Once is enough, and thank you for thinking of that. I'm glad one of us was making sure we didn't get too much too soon."

"You thought of it," she said, caressing his face with a loving touch that made him crazy for more of her. "Maybe this time next year, we'll be ready for a baby." She'd told him she wanted to be a young mother so she could fully enjoy the experience—and then fully enjoy her grandchildren someday.

"That sounds about right. I want you so bad, Mol. More than I've ever wanted anything in my whole life."

"More than the Beatles?"

He laughed. "They can't hold a candle to you."

"Wow, you must really love me."

"I really, really love you."

"Show me, Linc."

He was more than happy to, taking his time to kiss her until she was squirming under him, pressing against him, asking him for more. Moving down, he kissed her breasts and ran his tongue over the tight tips of her nipples.

She grasped his hair and cried out from the pleasure, which only made him harder than he already was for her.

Keeping up the slow seduction, he kissed her belly and her inner thighs, which quivered under his lips. "Are you cold?" he asked, his voice gruff with desire.

"Not even kinda."

Encouraged by her enthusiasm, he settled between her legs and gave her his tongue in deep, sweeping strokes that had her straining to get closer. When he slid two fingers into her heat and sucked on her clit, she came with a cry that took him right to the edge of his own release. God, she was sweet and responsive and loving and sexy and beautiful and smart and everything he'd ever wanted in one perfect package.

He moved up so he could see her face when he entered her for the first time.

Her eyes flew open, and her lips parted in a look of wonder that touched the deepest part of him.

"How did I ever get so lucky to find you in this crazy, massive world?" he asked.

"I don't know, but I'll always be thankful we found each other."

"Me too, love." With his arms around her, he entered her fully, seared by the heat and the pleasure and desire for more. He already knew he'd never get enough of how it felt to make love to Molly. As he moved in her, he watched her carefully, looking for ghosts or grief, but he saw only the same bliss he felt. "Are you okay?" he asked, just to be certain.

"Mmm, so much better than okay."

Her arms and legs encircled him, their bodies moving together like they'd been doing this forever. It shouldn't surprise him that even in this most intimate of moments, he felt more at home with her than he ever had with anyone else. It'd been that way with her from the beginning, from that first night at the bus station in Gulfport, when she'd looked up at him with the most adorable, arresting, interesting face he'd ever seen. That moment, he now knew, had changed both their lives forever, just as this one would, too, along with all the moments still to come.

His love for her fired a passion that was all new to him, as well as a desire to make her happy in every way, including this one. They got carried away on a wave of pleasure so intense, it threatened to consume them, when a loud pop followed by a hiss had them stopping short to realize the air mattress had burst.

And then they were laughing. They laughed so hard, they almost forgot what they'd been doing when the mattress exploded.

Almost...

Linc pushed into her as he gazed down at her face, awash with laughter and tears and happiness. This was, without any doubt in his mind, the best moment of his life, a thought he decided to share with her.

"It is for me, too. It'll take a lot to top this."

"I bet we can top it a million times."

"I'll take that bet."

"THE MATTRESS POPPING IS STILL THE BEST THING TO EVER happen," Molly said when they stopped laughing the way they always did any time they revisited their first night together.

"The second best was having to buy another one at the store and your dad asking me why we needed two of them. I had to think fast and tell him it was because we needed one for inside and one for the tent when we went camping. He gave me the foulest look that day, and I knew he was *dying* to tell me to keep my filthy hands off his little girl."

"His little girl loves your filthy hands and has the ten children to prove it."

"Don't tell him that. He still has the rifle."

"You haven't been afraid of him in a long time."

"True, but it's better if we don't tell him too much, even after all this time." He ran his fingers through her hair and thought back to that momentous day in which their lives together really began.

"Sometimes it's hard to believe everything that happened in that one day," she said.

"I know. The best and worst thing, all at once."

"I've always been so sorry you were forced to choose."

"You know, I've thought about that so much over the years."

"You hardly ever said anything."

"Eh, it's not like it was weighing me down on a daily basis or anything like that. After the first year or so, when I realized I wasn't going to hear from my mom or Char or the boys, I only thought about it in passing, like on holidays. I'd wonder what they were doing that day, or on one of their birthdays. But it occurred to me, after a while, that even if I hadn't met you, my father and I were headed for a falling-out, because I didn't want to work for his company."

"You can't be sure of that."

"I'm pretty sure it would've happened anyway. The problem I had before I met you was I didn't have a viable alternative that made sense to me, which meant I'd end up settling for the default, whether that's what I wanted or not. Once I met you and heard about your family's business and saw it for myself, I had found something that interested me. In a way, meeting you only accelerated the inevitable. The only regret I've ever had about any of it was that you were there to see it and that he treated you the way he did. I hate that that was the only interaction you've ever had with my family."

"It isn't really. I feel like I know them through the stories you've shared, like how you and your brothers would sail in the summers off the Jersey Shore, and the time you spent there with your grandparents, how your sister was your buddy growing up, how you suffered over the loss of Hunter. I've also heard you speak so lovingly of your mother at various times. My view of them isn't one-dimensional, Linc. If you loved them, I know there's more to them than what I saw that day."

"I hadn't thought of it that way, but I'm glad to know that's not the only point of reference you have. Can I make a confession that might sound so silly?"

"Of course."

"When I talked to Charlotte today, she said something that keeps running around in my mind."

"What's that?"

"She said that even if I don't go there to see my father, she hoped we can stay in touch going forward."

Molly's brows furrowed as she considered that. "Do you think that's the best idea? I mean, where's she been all this time?"

"I've decided I don't care where she's been or what he said to make her and my brothers afraid to find me or keep in touch with me. I just don't care. I want her back. I want my brothers back. I want them to know you and the kids, and I want to know their families. I don't *care* why they stayed away. I know in my heart it wasn't their choice, so what does it matter?"

"I hear what you're saying, and I understand why you feel the way you do. It's just that, well…"

"What, honey? You know I want your opinion."

"They *knew* where you were, Linc. Charlotte knew exactly where to find you when she needed to reach you today. Surely they weren't so under your father's thumb as fully grown adults that they couldn't have reached out before now."

"You're right," he said with a sigh, "and I'm sure they had their reasons for not getting in touch. All I'm saying is I don't care anymore why they didn't."

"Will you understand if I'm not so quick to forgive and forget?"

"Of course."

"I want to hear *why* they stayed away before I decide anything."

"Fair enough."

"You ought to get some sleep. Tomorrow will be a long day, and the day after will be, too."

The day after tomorrow, he would see his family again for the first time in forty years. His emotions were a mixed-up kettle of highs and lows, of memories, despair and hope. Among the many emotions, it was the hope that burned the brightest. More than anything, he hoped his father's dying request might reunite him with the siblings he'd loved and missed for such a long time.

CHAPTER FOURTEEN

"I love the past. There are parts of the past I hate, of course."
—Paul McCartney

*L*inc slept fitfully, dreaming of people he'd known as a boy, like his grandparents, his late brother Hunter, his other brothers and sister, his mother, aunts, uncles and cousins, all of whom had been lost to him in the family meltdown. He dreamed of Molly and their children, not as they were now, but as they'd been as little ones, running around and raising hell inside the barn they'd called home.

And then he was alone, walking on a mountain trail, looking for the others but not able to find them. He, who was always surrounded by a gaggle of people, wasn't sure how to be alone and didn't like the feeling.

He called out for Molly, for the kids…

Molly's voice cut through the roar of the wind, calling his name.

He opened his eyes to murky predawn darkness.

"You were dreaming," she said.

"Couldn't find you."

She snuggled up to him. "I'm right here, and it's still early. Try to go back to sleep."

Linc stared up at the ceiling, thinking about the journey into the past he would undertake later that day, and knew he'd never go back to sleep. He left Molly to rest for a while longer and got up to shower, shave, get dressed and pack an overnight bag for the trip. He was the first one to arrive at the office and was enjoying a cup of coffee and perusing the most outstanding sales reports he'd ever seen when the clock in the reception area chimed six o'clock.

Determined not to lose this entire day to the drama circulating around him, he dove into the monthly profit and loss statement that Hunter meticulously prepared and had started a list of questions for his CFO son by the time daylight began to creep through the blinds.

His stomach growled, and he decided to run across the street to get breakfast at the diner before it got busy. When he crossed Elm Street and entered the diner, he wasn't surprised to find his daughter-in-law Megan already there. Even eight months pregnant, she was never late for her morning shift, even when she'd suffered from morning sickness earlier in her pregnancy.

"Morning," she said, giving him a wary look. "What're you doing here so early?"

"Couldn't sleep, so I came in to get something done before we leave." Since it was just the two of them, he sat at the counter.

She poured him a cup of coffee and pushed the cream his way. "How're you doing?"

"Remarkably well, all things considered. Molly and the kids have been propping me up."

"I hope you know... I'm pretty sure I speak for everyone

when I say we think it's just *outrageous* that it happened in the first place."

"Thank you, honey. I appreciate that, but it was a long time ago. It has no bearing on my wonderful life or family."

"What do you feel like eating?"

"Is Butch here yet?" Linc asked, peering around her to see if the cook was in.

"He's due any minute."

"I'll wait for him. I don't want you cooking for me."

She rested her hand on top of his. "It would be my pleasure to make your usual for you, Linc."

He realized she wanted to do something for him. He turned his hand up to squeeze hers. "Then I gratefully accept. Thank you."

"Coming right up."

She turned the TV on to CNBC, handed him the morning's *Wall Street Journal* and refilled his coffee cup before heading to the kitchen to make his breakfast. How blessed he was, he thought, to be surrounded by so many people who loved him every day, but especially today when he was feeling so raw.

Linc flipped through the financial news in the paper, gave the market ticker on the TV a cursory glance and tried to keep his mind on all the things that usually framed his days—Molly, their family, friends, the various businesses the family ran, their community, the upcoming holiday—so he wouldn't be dragged into a rabbit hole of emotions.

If he tried to tell himself it was just another day, then he'd be okay. The silver lining, if there was such a thing to be found in this situation, was a night away with Molly and all their kids. Other than the trip to Boston earlier in the year for Wade's wedding, it'd been a while since they'd traveled anywhere together as a group. They'd done a lot of camping when their family was young, mostly because that was the only thing they could afford for their family of twelve, not to mention the various pets who'd tagged along on their adventures.

In recent years, they'd added a number of daughters- and sons-in-law, as well as significant others, fiancés and grandchildren that had taken the original twelve to...

Taking the pen Megan had left on the counter, he made a list on a napkin:

Hunter, Megan
Hannah, Nolan, Callie
Will, Cameron, Chase
Ella, Gavin
Charley, Tyler
Wade, Mia
Colton, Lucy
Lucas, Dani, Savannah
Landon, Amanda, Stella
Max, Caden

A total of twenty-seven, counting him, Molly and Elmer, with four more on the way. He was glad he'd done that math. It was a number he looked forward to sharing with his father after he introduced him to the ten grandchildren he'd never know thanks to the ultimatum that had come between the two of them.

Having been a grandfather for a year now, he actually pitied his father for what his stubborn rigidness had caused him to miss with Linc's kids. The whole thing was unbearably sad. One of the questions he'd frequently pondered over the years was how things might've been different for him—for all of them—if his brother Hunter hadn't died. That'd been the start of their downward spiral as a family with the scene in his father's study their rock bottom.

The bells on the door jingled, jarring Linc from his

thoughts about the past. He glanced over his shoulder to see his father-in-law come in, shivering from the cold.

"You're up early," Linc said.

Elmer slid onto the stool next to Linc. "Could say the same to you."

"I'm not sure I actually slept more than an hour or two last night."

"Got a lot on your mind, son."

"Indeed."

"I was thinking last night about that day when the two of you came home from Philly, shell-shocked."

"And Molly… She just took care of it, didn't she?"

Elmer smiled. "She sure did."

"Tell me the truth. Did you want to say no when she asked you to marry us that night?" They'd never talked about it again, and only the four of them had ever known it had happened.

Elmer got up, went behind the counter and poured himself a cup of coffee and then topped off Linc's mug. "Truth?"

"Nothing but."

"It never occurred to me to say no to her. By then, I knew for certain you were what she wanted, and you'd shown me at work that you weren't faking your interest in her family business. And when I heard your father had given you that awful ultimatum and you'd walked away from everything else that mattered to you so you could marry my Molly…" He shrugged. "Suffice to say I was honored to preside over both your weddings."

"Wait," Megan said as she came from the kitchen with Linc's breakfast. "You had *two* weddings?"

Elmer grimaced at Linc. "Sorry."

"It's okay. The only reason we never talked about the first one with the kids was that we'd have to tell them what else had happened that day, and I didn't want them to know."

Megan put the plate in front of Linc and automatically put a bottle of the hot sauce he sometimes liked on eggs on the counter. He loved how she did those things without even thinking, tending to the likes and dislikes of her many customers automatically.

"Thank you, honey. And yes, Molly and I had two weddings, but no one really knows that except the two of us and her parents."

"Oh," she said with a gleeful grin, "so I know something none of the kids know?"

"Yes, you do," Linc said, amused by her delight in having a scoop. "The day my father issued the ultimatum?"

Megan nodded.

"We came home to Vermont, and Molly asked her dad to marry us right away. It was like she knew I needed that after what'd occurred earlier. She was amazing that night. So determined to do whatever she could to show me I still had a family."

"I love that," Megan said, sighing. "*So* romantic."

"It was pretty awesome," Linc said, smiling as he remembered that night and the incident with the air mattress. That was something that belonged only to him and Molly.

"Will you tell the others about that now that they know the rest?"

"I suppose maybe we should so they can hear just how incredible their mom was and is."

"They already know that," Megan said. "This'll just elevate her to cult status."

"Where she belongs," Elmer said.

Linc nodded. "Couldn't agree more." When he stood to leave the diner a short time later, Megan came around the counter to hug him.

"I hope it goes as well as possible, and please know that those of us who aren't there will be back here wishing you the best. We all love you, Linc."

Linc returned her hug. "Thank you, honey. Love you, too. Hold down the fort for us around here while we're gone."

"Will do."

"And don't tell Butch I said so, but your eggs are better than his."

"Oh my God! I'm *so* telling him that!"

Laughing, Linc left the diner, crossed the street and headed up the stairs to the office, where Emma greeted him with a worried look. "Morning, and yes, I'm okay."

"Glad to hear it. I was sorry to hear what you're going through, but I'm glad your family has rallied around you, not that it surprises me."

"I'm a very lucky man, and nothing that happens in the next twenty-four hours can change that."

"I wish you the best of luck on the trip. I hope you know that."

"I do, and I appreciate it very much. I'm going to see if I can get something done before we leave."

"Sounds good."

Seeing that none of the kids were in yet, Linc went into his office and shut the door, wanting to make a call before everyone else arrived. No doubt they'd be sticking close to him that day, and he wouldn't have it any other way.

As he dialed the numbers, he was angry with himself for being nervous, but it was only the second time in forty years he'd called his sister. It was only natural to be nervous. The phone rang three times before a man's voice answered.

"Hello, this is Lincoln Abbott calling for Charlotte. Is she available?"

After a long pause, the man said, "One moment, please."

In the background, he heard the man say, "Char, for you. Your brother. Lincoln."

Char. Hearing the familiar nickname gave him a pang. That's what he'd called her growing up.

"Lincoln? Are you there?"

"I'm here."

"I'm so glad you called. I was hoping you would."

"I wanted to let you know I'll be there to see Father tomorrow morning around ten, if that's all right."

"That should be fine. He's better in the mornings."

"Will I see you, too?"

"I wouldn't miss it for anything."

"I'll see you then."

"Safe travels, Linc."

He put down the phone and sat for a long time, letting his mind wander to a childhood filled with good times with his mother, siblings, cousins and grandparents. His father had worked—a lot—so they hadn't seen as much of him, especially during the summers when they decamped to his grandparents' place on the shore.

Those had been idyllic days until they lost Hunter and everything had changed for all of them, and particularly for him, who'd suddenly become the heir apparent to the family business his brother had been groomed to lead. After Hunter died, it became clear to Linc that his father expected him to take his brother's place in the company. They'd never actually discussed it. Rather, it'd been understood, one more thing that changed amid the shock and grief of his brother's sudden death.

A knock sounded on the door he rarely closed. "Dad?"

"Come in."

His late brother's namesake came in, tall, dark, handsome and smarter than Linc would ever be. "Morning, son."

"How're you doing?"

"I'm all right. You?"

"Same." Hunter took a seat on the other side of his father's desk. "Is there anything I can do for you?"

"No, but thank you for asking." He looked at his firstborn, who definitely bore a familial resemblance to his late uncle. "I was just thinking about my brother, the one you were named for."

"I was curious about him after you mentioned him."

Linc nodded. "Losing him was the worst thing to ever happen. He was an expert sailor. No one could explain how it was possible that something like that could happen to him. It's one of those things we'll just never know."

"I'm so sorry you lost him that way."

"Thank you. He was supposed to run the company. And after we lost him…"

"Your father turned to you."

"Yes. Only, Hunter wanted it, and I didn't."

"Did your father know that?"

"He did, but that didn't matter. His father had started the company, handed it down to him, and it was coming my way whether I wanted it or not."

"That's a heavy thing to put on someone so young."

"It was, and sometimes I felt like an ungrateful jerk for wanting something different, even if I didn't know yet what that different thing was. More than anything, I didn't want my entire life decided for me before I was twenty-five."

"I can certainly understand that. What was it about this place that interested you when that didn't?"

"The potential," Linc said. "That was the first thing I saw when I came here, that it could be so much more than it already was. Gramps would tell you he was guilty of doing things a certain way because that was the way they'd always been done. I tried to show him another way, and for a while, he fought me. He's not big on change."

"He and I have that in common."

Linc cracked up. "That's a fact. I like that we sell a way of life here, a simpler way, and people connect with that. We're all nostalgic for simpler times in our lives, and in our fast-paced world, we give our customers something different. I've said from the beginning that the potential here is limited only by our own imaginations."

"You got the new P&L, right?"

"I did."

"I guess it's safe to say you were right about the catalog and the intimate line."

Linc smiled. "Had a feeling I would be. I've been wanting to do the catalog for twenty years. Just took a while for all the pieces to come together."

"The business is on the verge of exploding, Dad. Like exploding to a level we never saw coming. Or I should say, a level the rest of us never saw coming."

"That's a very good problem to have."

"Indeed, but one we're going to have to manage."

"Let's talk about that after the holidays."

CHAPTER FIFTEEN

"I believe time wounds all heels."
—John Lennon

*M*olly waited until nine o'clock, when she was sure her sister would be up and at work as the Butler town clerk. Her office was attached to her home, and Molly often stopped by for coffee and a chat while Hannah was working.

When she pulled into Hannah's driveway, she was surprised to see the closed sign on the door to the clerk's office and Ray Mulvaney's SUV parked in the driveway. *Well, well, well*, Molly thought. Good for them. Her sister had been alone for years after Mike left her, and no one was more thrilled for her and Ray than Molly.

The last thing she wanted to do was interrupt anything, but damn it, she needed her sister, one of the few people in the world who knew most of what'd gone on during that memorable week forty years ago. She went up the stairs to the mudroom door and knocked. When Hannah didn't answer, she rang the doorbell.

A few minutes later, Hannah came to the door, wearing a bathrobe and attempting to straighten her hair. "Hey." She opened the door for Molly. "Come in."

"You're not working today?"

"Later. I had a council meeting that went until midnight."

"I woke you up. I'm sorry. Go back to bed."

"It's okay. I was awake." Hannah got busy making coffee. "What's got you out so early?"

"You won't believe it if I told you."

Hannah glanced at Molly over her shoulder. "Is everyone all right?"

"Yes, but apparently, we're going to Philadelphia today."

"You and Linc?"

"And the kids."

"*All* of them?"

"All of them." Molly took off her coat and sat at the kitchen table. "Where's Ray?"

"In the shower, I think."

"It's progressed to sleepovers and showers, has it?"

"A while ago, actually."

"I should go. You guys were having a morning, and I interrupted."

"It's fine. I wanted to talk to you anyway, but you first." She brought mugs of steaming coffee to the table, along with cream and sugar. "Tell me about Philly."

Molly stirred cream into her coffee and told Hannah about Linc's sister calling.

"Holy shit," Hannah said, wide-eyed. "She called to tell him their father is dying and wants to see him. And now you're going there."

"We're going there."

"When?"

"Today."

"Three days before Christmas?"

"His sister said their father doesn't have much time."

"Damn."

"I'm so *angry*, Han. That they can call him after forty years and ask this of him. I'm trying to be supportive of him, but all I feel is the anger."

"Can't say I blame you. What they did was monstrous."

"I want to kidnap him and drive him north to Canada or somewhere they can't get to him until that craven old man is gone and can't hurt him anymore."

"You know you could do that if you were so inclined. Tell him you want to show him something, get in the car and head north."

Molly dropped her head into her hands. "I'm sorely tempted." She looked up at Hannah. "What right do they have to do this to him after *forty* years?"

"They have no right at all."

Ray came into the kitchen and stopped short when he saw Molly there, glancing at Hannah as if he wasn't sure what to do.

Hannah reached out her hand to him. "It's okay. She knows you sleep over."

"Oh, um… Well…"

Molly laughed at his befuddled response and the way his handsome face turned bright red. "Sorry to interrupt your morning."

"You didn't," Ray said. "Can I make you ladies some breakfast?"

"And he cooks, *too*," Hannah said with a smug grin. To Ray, she said, "That'd be lovely. Thank you."

"Coming right up."

When Ray was occupied with cooking, Molly leaned in to whisper to her sister, "*Go*, girl."

"Right?" Hannah lowered her voice even further. "I'm thinking about asking him to move in."

"Is that right?"

Hannah shrugged. "He's here every night anyway."

Ray poured himself a cup of coffee. "I can hear you two talking about me."

"We're not talking about you," Hannah said. "We're talking about my other boyfriend, the one you don't know about."

"Sure you are. That's all right. I'll still make you breakfast even if you're talking about me."

"We're actually talking about how Linc's family contacted him for the first time in forty years and asked him to come to his father's deathbed so the father can make himself feel better about cutting him off before he dies." She glanced at Molly. "Did I get that right?"

"Spot-on."

"That's extremely screwed up," Ray said.

"You don't know the half of it," Hannah replied.

"What's he going to do?" Ray asked.

"I guess we're going there so his father can clear his conscience before he dies," Molly said.

"And three days before Christmas, no less," Hannah said. "I'm sorry you guys have to deal with this, Mols. Are you going to drive or fly?"

"We're driving. The kids want to be there to support their father and, as Hunter put it so perfectly, to let their grandfather see what came of this marriage and life he was so opposed to."

"That's lovely," Hannah said with a sigh. "Good for them."

"I guess I should go home and pack."

"Look at it this way—it's a rare opportunity to get away with your kids. How often does that happen anymore?"

"Not very."

"Try to enjoy it, because you know that mixed in with the emotion will be a lot of laughs."

"Probably."

"Definitely. We're talking about your kids. They're nothing if not funny."

"They are," Molly said with a smile.

"They'll get you through this, and you'll come home to Christmas. It'll be fine."

"Will he be fine? Linc?"

"Of course he will. He has you and your incredible family to get him through it. This is a blip. He'll deal with it and go on with his life."

"I hope you're right." Molly stood to leave. "Thanks for listening to me whine."

"You're not whining. You're understandably furious."

"I am, but Linc doesn't need to see that."

"That's what sisters are for." Hannah hugged her. "Hang in there."

"Thanks, Han. Appreciate this so much."

"Any time."

Ray came over and handed her something warm wrapped in a paper towel. "Egg sandwich to go."

Molly went up on tiptoes to kiss his cheek. "You're the best. Take good care of my sister."

"I'm trying, but she doesn't make it easy."

"Trust me, I know."

"Hush, you two. I can hear you."

"Come over after dinner on Christmas," Molly said. "We'll be home all day. And tell your kids, too."

"We'll see you at some point. Safe travels."

Molly got in her car and ate her delicious breakfast on the way home to the barn, where she'd pack and put on a happy face for this trip, even if she was seething on the inside. Linc was the best guy she'd ever known, other than her own father, and when he hurt, she hurt. The call from his sister hurt him. The request from his father hurt him.

If they said or did anything else to hurt him, Molly wouldn't be responsible for her actions.

HANNAH SHUT THE DOOR BEHIND HER SISTER AND TURNED TO watch Ray move around the kitchen like a pro. Wanting to be self-sufficient, he'd learned to cook after his wife died, he'd told her. After more than twenty years on her own since her husband left, Hannah was still getting used to having a man around again. But Ray made it easy on her. He didn't pressure her for more than she was willing to give or ask for things she wasn't sure she wanted.

Rather, he was patient and kind and sweet and loving and everything she could ask for in a partner, which was why she was on the verge of doing something she'd once sworn she'd never do again—make a commitment to a man.

She went to him and wrapped her arms around him from behind, resting her head on his back. He was rock solid from years of working construction, and the first thing he'd done after moving to Vermont to live near his daughters and granddaughter was join a gym so he wouldn't "go to hell in a handbasket," as he put it.

"What's up?" he asked in the gruff, New York-tinged voice she'd grown to love.

"Nothing much. What's up with you?"

"Well, I've got this sweet, sexy lady clinging to me, so something else will be 'up' if this continues."

And he was funny. Hannah had laughed more with him than she had since her kids had lived at home and kept her constantly entertained. "I'm happy you're here."

"Well, that's nice to hear. Will you let me go so I can turn around and have this conversation face-to-face with you?"

"I'd rather do it this way."

"We're not hiding anymore, remember?"

Hannah reluctantly let him go and stepped back to give him room to turn around.

He caressed her face, a loving, tender gesture that made her knees feel weak. That happened a lot when he was around. "What's on your mind, sweetheart?"

She looked up at his handsome face, weathered from years of working in the elements in New York City. "Thank you for being so patient with me."

"You've made it well worth the patience," he said with a suggestive grin.

Hannah felt her face go hot with embarrassment as she recalled their passionate nights together. He'd been a revelation to her, after having only been with her ex-husband. With Ray, she'd discovered that her marriage had been lacking in more ways than she'd realized.

He kissed her cheek and then her lips. "I love making you blush."

"You do it far too often."

"Because I love it so much." He kissed her neck and gave a gentle bite that had her gasping from the sensations that lit up her entire body. "You know I love *you*, Hannah, don't you?"

Hearing words that hadn't been spoken before, she went completely still. Her first inclination was to pull back, to retreat, to run from the potential of being hurt even worse than she had been before.

"Don't do that. Don't go back into your shell and hide from me."

"Old habits are hard to break."

"You don't need to do that anymore, Hannah. I already swore to you I'd never do to you what Mike did."

"Leave me alone with eight kids to finish raising?" she

asked with a small grin, looking for some levity as the conversation took a serious turn.

"Leave you ever."

"You can't know that."

"I do know that. I was alone for a long time after my wife died. I never imagined anything like this happening again for me, but then there you were, and here we are, and this is what I want. You're what I want." He tipped her chin up. "Admit you love me, too."

She shrugged. "Maybe a little."

His brows furrowed into an expression that had probably made his daughters, Lucy and Emma, quake when he'd directed it their way as children. It only made Hannah want to giggle because she knew she had nothing at all to fear from him. "Tell me the truth."

As she looked at the face that'd become the center of her life over the last year, she couldn't deny how she felt about him. "Yes, Ray, of course I love you, but I promised myself a long time ago I'd never again risk more than I could bear to lose."

"You're not risking anything with me but a lifetime of happiness. That's all I want for you—and for myself."

Hannah wanted that so badly, but in the back of her mind —always—was the lingering damage Mike had inflicted when he abruptly left her after nearly twenty years of marriage. Even after all this time, it still rankled her that she hadn't seen the end of her marriage coming until it was too late.

"I'll never do to you what he did, Hannah," he said again. "You already know that about me."

She did know that. Ray was as true blue as it got. He meant what he said, and his word was gold.

"Our kids…" Her Grayson would soon marry his Emma,

and a mess between her and Ray would be a mess for them, as well.

"Are madly in love and thrilled they led us to each other. You know that, too."

"I do, but if things were to go wrong between us—"

Ray kissed her. "Nothing's gonna go wrong."

"You say that now."

"I say that forever."

"I won't marry you."

He feigned offense. "I'm not asking you to, but I did hear you whisper to your sister that you're thinking about asking me to move in. So why don't you go ahead and do that?"

"Why would I want you to move in with me when you're such a pain in the ass?"

"Because I'm a great cook and a god in bed?"

"Oh my Lord," she said, rolling her eyes as she tried not to laugh her ass off.

"Am I wrong?"

"I refuse to answer that on the grounds you'll use it against me forever."

"You're using the word 'forever,' which is a good sign." He framed her face, kissed her again and compelled her to look up at him. "Ask me, Hannah. I promise you'll never regret it."

She already knew she wouldn't regret it, but the fear loomed larger than it ought to. "I have to tell you something first."

He looked at her warily. "What's that?"

"Mike called me last week."

"What'd he want?"

"To tell me that he's in remission thanks to Gray donating bone marrow to him, and he's been doing a lot of thinking and reflecting on his mistakes. The biggest of which, I guess, has to do with me and the children he left without a backward glance."

"So he's found religion after his life-threatening illness, has he?"

"Something like that. The kids have told me he's reached out to them, too."

"Why was he calling you?"

"To ask if I might be in a forgiving mood."

Ray's expression turned stormy. "*Is he for real?* More than twenty years after he split, he's coming back to sniff around? I hope you told him to fuck off."

She'd never heard him curse, let alone drop an F bomb. "I didn't say it that way, but I let him know my door is closed and padlocked. To him, anyway."

"Good," he said, settling somewhat. "Takes some nerve to come back with his tail between his legs after all this time, just because he thought he was going to die and finally decided to take stock of his shit decisions."

"You're very cute when you're pissed."

"I must be downright adorable right now, then." He put his hands on her shoulders and looked her in the eye. "Listen, Hannah. You already know I'm a simple kind of guy. I'm never going to overwhelm you with fancy words or grand gestures or romantic nonsense. What you get with me is as simple as I am: love, honesty, faithfulness, family, companionship, laughter and a promise that I won't split when it gets tough, which it certainly will at some point. All I need to be happy is to wake up with you, see my daughters just about every day, get my baby girl Simone off the school bus every afternoon, help her with her homework and then come home to have dinner with you before we go to bed together. If that's what every day for the rest of my life looked like, maybe with a few more grandkids thrown in at some point, it'd be way more than enough for me."

"And you said you wouldn't overwhelm me with fancy words," she said, ridiculously moved.

He scowled. "There was nothing fancy about that."

"And yet it was the fanciest thing anyone has ever said to me, because you mean it."

"Hell yes, I mean it. It's long past time you knew how terrific you are, how sweet, caring, loving, sexy and perfect. It's a goddamned shame your husband ever made you feel anything other than cherished, especially after you gave him the incredible gift of eight beautiful kids. The man ought to be taken out to the woodshed and horsewhipped for what he did."

"Your words are getting fancier."

"Shut up and ask me to move in with you."

"You're being kind of pushy, aren't you?" she asked, amused.

"Ask me, Hannah."

She gave him a coy look she wouldn't have thought herself still capable of before he showed her the many things she was still capable of. "You wanna move in?"

"Hell yes. I thought you'd never ask."

"You promise you won't make me sorry I did, right?"

"Swear to God."

That, Hannah decided as she melted into his fierce embrace, was about the best guarantee she could ever hope to receive.

CHAPTER SIXTEEN

"Everything will be okay in the end.
If it's not okay, it's not the end."
—John Lennon

*A*fter a busy morning in the office and in the store, with everyone making sure their areas of the business were covered for the time they'd be gone, the family loaded up a smaller bus than the one they'd taken to Boston in June. Car seats were strapped in for Callie and Caden, snacks were provided by Ella and Charley, and, as usual, Lucas and Landon were the last ones to arrive, right when Linc was threatening to leave without them.

"Sorry," Landon said as he preceded his brother onto the bus. "It was his fault we're late. I had to pry him away from Dani with a crowbar."

"Oh my God," Lucas said. "Shut up, will you?"

"Both of you shut up, and sit your asses down so we can get going," Molly said.

"Mom said *shut up*," Landon said, scandalized.

Those words had been on Molly's list of felony offenses in the barn when they were growing up.

"You buffoons drive me to it," Molly said, making everyone else laugh.

That's good, Linc thought. *The laughs will help me get through this, and there are sure to be plenty of laughs when this group goes somewhere together.* Before he gave the signal to Bill, the driver, to depart, Linc stood and faced the people he loved the most. "I just want to say thanks for this. I know the timing is awful with Christmas this week, but it means the world to me that you all insisted on coming."

"There's no way we'd let you do this without us, Dad," Hannah said, "so let's get going so we can get back home to enjoy Christmas."

"You heard the lady," Linc said to Bill. "Let's go to Philly."

Hunter had ensured the movie system on the bus had their favorite holiday movie, *Christmas Vacation*, cued up for the ride, and as he listened to his family laugh and shout the iconic quotes, Linc could only smile at the way they always came through for him.

"Funny that the traumatic call from Philly is going to give us one of the most memorable Christmases in years, isn't it?" Molly quietly asked him.

"I was thinking the same thing."

"When was the last time, other than the wedding, that we all went somewhere together like this?"

"It's been a *long* time," he said, "and back then, we had to take two cars because you had so many kids."

"Yes, that was all my fault."

"One hundred percent your fault for being a fertile Myrtle."

They'd had this "fight" for years about who was ultimately responsible for them having ten kids.

"Remember after we had Colton and we said seven was more than enough?" Molly asked.

"I sure do."

"And then somehow, a few years later, you managed to knock me up *again* with twins. You're lucky I didn't murder you then."

"I can't help it that you're powerless to resist me, or that your eggs were always so *welcoming* to my boys."

Molly sputtered with laughter. "Shut up with your prowess and your boys."

"Is it or is it not the truth?"

From behind them, Will leaned forward. "I have no idea what you two are talking about, and let me be crystal clear—I don't *want* to know. But I'm hearing enough to plead with you, for the love of God, to *change the subject*."

Molly rocked with silent laughter.

"It's your mother's fault, William," Linc said. "She's always been this way. I did my best to try to manage her, but you saw how that went. Ten children later…"

"Oh, stuff it, Lincoln Abbott."

And so it went for seven hours full of family, fun, arguments over who initiated the most pit stops—Charley—and who farted—Colton, Lucas and Landon in a competition for volume and stink that had everyone screaming and opening the windows to frigid air—and in-depth discussions about where they ought to stop for dinner. They settled on a roadside steak house in New Jersey.

They arrived at their hotel shortly after eleven. Hunter took care of the check-in using Linc's credit card and returned with room keys.

"Hannah, you and Callie are with me," Hunter said. "Will, you're with Wade."

"Thank you for not giving me Colton," Will said.

"Max gets him," Hunter said.

173

"What'd I do to piss you off?" Max asked to laughter from the others.

Hunter handed Max his key. "Sorry, pal, but someone has to take one for the team."

"I made sure to double down on the beans at dinner," Colton said.

"I have a *child*," Max reminded his brother. "Who needs to breathe *fresh* air. Can't we leave Colton on the bus?"

"There's no law that says we can't, right, Mol?" Linc asked.

"Not that I know of."

"I'm not staying on the bus," Colton said indignantly.

"Then I need a cork." Max carried Caden as he followed Colton off the bus. "A very large cork."

"Lucas and Landon are together, and Ella and Gavin," Hunter said, handing them keycards.

Charley pumped her fist in the air. "That leaves me with my own room."

"You get Gramps," Hunter said, handing keys to her and Elmer.

"Sorry to disappoint you, Charley," Elmer said, grinning.

"You're the only one I'd want, Gramps," Charley said, hooking her arm through his. "Best roommate ever."

Hunter gestured for his parents to go ahead of him off the bus.

"Thank you for wrangling this unruly crew, son," Linc said.

"My pleasure. For the most part, anyway."

"We get it," Molly said, smiling at their eldest. "We know how it goes."

"In light of the reason for the mission, is it weird to think this is actually kind of fun?" Hunter asked.

"Not at all," Linc said. "We were saying the same thing earlier.

It's a rare moment when the original twelve get to do anything like this. Even when we went to Boston, Wade wasn't with us. I suppose we can thank my father for giving us a good excuse."

"Nah, we aren't giving him credit for anything other than your life," Hunter said. "For that, we shall always be thankful. Otherwise, he can go fuck himself."

Linc laughed. "I can live with that. You took care of Bill, right?"

"Yep. He's the only one who gets his own room."

"Excellent. Thank you."

"Let's get some sleep," Hunter said. "And just remember—no matter how difficult tomorrow may be, nothing that matters will change."

Linc squeezed his son's shoulder. "That's a very comforting thought, son. And it's true." Lincoln followed Molly and Hunter off the bus and into the hotel. They took the elevator to the fourth floor.

"I hope we have this floor to ourselves," Linc said when they stepped off the elevator into a low hum of voices and laughter.

"I mentioned to the reservations people that they might want to give us our own area since we're known for being loud."

"Good call," Linc said. "We'll see you in the morning."

"Sleep well," Hunter said.

Linc opened the door, ushered Molly in ahead of him and carried both their bags as he followed her into the spacious room with a king-size bed.

Molly sat on the bed to test its firmness.

"How is it?"

"Very good. You know how I feel about hotels."

"I do indeed. I believe Charley *and* Wade were the result of hotel stays."

"Remember how we used to leave the older kids with Mom and Dad and run for our lives to a hotel for the night?"

"Do I ever. And wasn't it just our luck that we'd come home with even *more* kids?"

"It took us a while to figure out where they were coming from, and by the time we did, we had ten of them."

"And thank goodness for that. I can't imagine life without any of them."

"You say that now that we're empty nesters. For a while, you wanted to sell them all to the circus."

"That's true," Linc said, unbuttoning his shirt. "I would've actually given them away for a few years there."

"It was fun, though, wasn't it? Even during the crazy years?"

"Always fun, and even more so now that they've grown up to be outstanding adults."

"With the manners, at times, of the cows who used to live in our barn."

"That might be an insult to the cows." Linc sat next to her on the foot of the bed and put his arm around her. "Despite the farting contest and the fact that Colton can sing the national anthem in burps, we did good, didn't we?"

"We did great, and that's what your dad will see tomorrow, Linc. He'll see a man who grew into a smashing success in all the ways that matter most. He'll see an outstanding husband, father, grandfather, uncle and businessman. He'll see that you thrived in spite of him."

"You always did make me look good, Molly Stillman."

"We make each other look good. None of this happens without both of us, and frankly, I can't wait for him to meet our ten beautiful children and see what he missed out on."

Her fiercely spoken words made him love her so damned much. "Want to try for number eleven?" he asked, using his regular pickup line because it always got a laugh out of her.

"Absolutely, but tell the boys no more doubles."

"I'll let them know."

By the time the bus pulled up in front of Lincoln's childhood home at ten o'clock the next morning, he felt ready for whatever was about to happen. Each of his children had hugged him after breakfast in a show of support that'd nearly reduced him to tears.

Their message was clear: They had his back.

And knowing that made this day a thousand times easier than it would have been without them following him up the stairs to the door, which swung open before he could ring the bell.

Charlotte.

He would've known her anywhere, despite the signs of aging that forty years wrought. She wore her silvery hair in the same short bob she'd favored as a younger woman, and her blue eyes sparkled with pleasure at the sight of him. Because he couldn't remain aloof even if he wanted to, he hugged her.

"It's so, *so* good to see you, Linc," she said before doing a double take at the crowd he'd brought with him.

"This is my family," he said as they followed him into a spacious foyer that brought back a thousand and one memories of his childhood in this house. "You remember Molly. And these are our kids." He pointed to each of them, and they waved as he introduced them. "Wade, Colton, Lucas, Landon, Max, Hunter, Ella, Charley, Hannah and Will, and two of our grandchildren, Caden and Callie, our son-in-law, Gavin, and Molly's father, Elmer. Everyone, this is my sister, Charlotte."

"I lost count," Charlotte said, seeming stunned. "Eight?"

"Ten," Linc said with a proud smile. "Including two sets of twins, Hunter and Hannah and Lucas and Landon."

"Wow." Charlotte seemed overwhelmed as she shook hands with her nieces and nephews, while Linc wanted to wail at the absurdity of her meeting them for the first time as adults. "It's so nice to meet you all."

The kids were too polite not to return her handshake, but their responses were muted and lacked their usual enthusiasm for new people. Of course, only Linc, Molly and Elmer would know that.

"We weren't expecting a crowd," Charlotte said, retaining her friendly, welcoming demeanor. "I had no idea… The website for the store only shows five."

It pleased him greatly that she'd cared enough to look.

"Five are actively involved in the day-to-day operations. Hunter is our CFO, Will oversees our Vermont Made line, Wade is our health and wellness expert, Charley is in IT, and Ella manages the sales team. The others contribute products and services to the family business. Colton and Max run our maple syrup operation, Landon oversees the Christmas tree farm, Hannah makes jewelry, and Lucas makes furniture and other designs that are sold in the store. Everyone contributes to the business Elmer's parents founded."

"You had said it was a store… I had no idea it was so much more than that."

"It's a ten-million-dollar-a-year operation and growing thanks to the addition of a catalog earlier this year that's exploded our revenue," Hunter said.

"Hunter is the CFO for all our businesses," Linc said proudly.

"You named your son Hunter."

"I did. And my daughter Charlotte and my other sons Will and Max. I never forgot about any of you, Char, even if you forgot about me."

She gasped. "We *never* forgot about you."

"Where've you been all this time, Charlotte?" Molly asked, because Linc was too tongue-tied to do it. "You've known where to find Lincoln. What kept you away?"

"I thought... We were sure we wouldn't be welcome."

"You knew that wasn't true," Linc said.

"We should've stopped what happened that day," Charlotte said. "We should've marched in there and told him if he was kicking you out of the family, we were going with you. But we didn't do that. We let him do what he did, and after that..." She shrugged. "We wouldn't want to see us, so we figured you didn't either. Max and I always regretted that we didn't do more that day."

"But I wrote to you. All of you. For years. I told you I wanted to see you."

Her expression flattened with shock. "You *wrote* to us? Here?"

He nodded. "Every month. For ten years."

"I never... I didn't get those letters. None of us did." Her eyes filled with tears. "How could he do this to us?"

"We may never know that," Linc said, "and frankly, it doesn't matter now. What matters is we both know that the other always would've been welcome, and that's all we need to know."

"Yes, I suppose that's true, although I find it hard to believe it could be that simple."

"It is that simple, Char. We've been denied each other's presence for forty years. That's long enough, isn't it?"

"More than long enough." With tears sliding down her cheeks, she hugged him as two other men joined them in the foyer.

Linc pulled back from his sister to greet his brothers, Will and Max, both of them sporting the same gray hair and blue eyes he had and wide smiles for their older brother.

"Is it really you?" Will asked.

"It's me." Linc hugged them both. "And I'm so happy to see you."

"What's with the baseball team you brought with you?" Will asked with a teasing grin.

"He has *ten* children," Char said.

"That's our Linc," Max said. "Always the overachiever."

"This is my family." Linc went through the introductions once again. "I only brought half of the immediate family."

His siblings' laughter took Linc right back to a thousand memories of growing up with the three of them as well as their Hunter. "Does Father know I'm coming?"

Char shook her head. "We didn't tell him in case you changed your mind at the last minute. None of us would've blamed you if you had."

"It's incredibly good of you to come," Will said bluntly. "I'm not sure I would have."

"Time has a way of dulling the edges of things that happened decades ago," Linc said. "He asked me to come. I came." He put his arm around Molly. "He doesn't mean anything to me anymore. As you can see—and he will see— I've never once regretted the choice he forced me to make, even if I missed you all very much."

"We never forgave him for what he did to you," Max said fiercely. "It wasn't the same between us and him. We refused to work for the company, and he ended up selling it about twelve years ago."

Linc took an almost perverse satisfaction in hearing that his siblings had taken that stand, but it pained him that his father's line in the sand had been for nothing. So many people hurt for no good reason.

"He wrote to us," Char told their brothers. "Every month for ten years."

Max's mouth fell open before it snapped shut. "God damn him."

"I would've liked to have gotten those letters," Will said softly, his devastation apparent.

"Let's put it in the past where it belongs," Linc said. "He took us from each other for forty years. What happens next is up to us. And to start with, I want to know about you guys. Married? Kids? What've you done with yourselves?"

"Let's go sit so we can talk for a minute," Char said.

CHAPTER SEVENTEEN

"Take these broken wings and learn to fly."
—Paul McCartney

*H*is sister led the way into the family room, which had been redone since Linc was last there. The fireplace and built-in bookshelves were as he remembered and still full of books. Both his parents had been big readers and had passed the hobby along to their children.

His family surrounded him, some sitting on sofas and chairs, and others standing behind him.

"I married Andy Higgins," Char said.

"No way!" Andy had been one of Linc's closest friends as a child. "When did that happen?"

"A few years after…"

After his banishment, she meant. "Kids?"

"Four," Char said. "Two of each, including a son named Lincoln."

"Oh," Linc said, incredibly moved. "Well… That's lovely."

"We never forgot you either," she said with a sigh. "I'm the executive director of a nonprofit that helps to place formerly homeless women in new careers."

"I can see that for you," Linc said. His sister had always been tuned in to the needs of those less fortunate than they had been.

"I'm a dentist," Will said, "married to Kendall, and we have three daughters."

"My wife, Courtney, and I have twin sons," Max said. "I work for a tech company that supports cell phone networks."

"Wow, three sets of twins between us," Linc said to his brother. "I want to see pictures of my nieces and nephews."

"We could use your services in Butler, Vermont," Landon said to his uncle Max. "The place cell service went to die."

"You don't have cell service there?" Uncle Max asked, seeming stunned that anyone lived without such a modern luxury.

"Nope," Linc said. "I've never owned a cell phone."

"I can't wrap my head around this," Uncle Max said.

"You sound like my wife, Cameron," Will said.

"And mine," Colton added. "Cam and Lucy lived in New York City until they moved to Butler. It was a bit of an adjustment, to say the least."

The conversation took off from there as his siblings shared photos of their families with him, and his kids conversed with their aunt and uncles, who'd apparently said enough to earn the forgiveness of his crew. That made Linc happy. He was ready to forgive and move on, even if he'd never forget.

A short time later, Linc looked over at his sister. "I suppose I should see Father."

"I can take you up."

"I want him to see Molly and the kids." He borrowed Hunter's words when he said, "I want him to see what came of the ultimatum he gave me."

"I think he should see that, too. Let me take you to him."

As they followed Char up the stairs, Molly took Linc's hand and gave it a squeeze. He glanced at her, and the warm smile she directed his way calmed and settled him. No matter what happened in the next few minutes, when he went to bed tonight it would be with her, and forty years of sleeping next to her was worth any sacrifice he'd had to make.

More memories flooded his mind as he went up the familiar stairs to the second floor. At the landing, he looked to the closed door on the left that had been his bedroom. He wondered what they'd done with his things.

"Let me tell him you're here," Char said, stepping into the master bedroom at the end of the hallway.

From outside the door, Linc could hear his sister say, "Father, Lincoln is here. He's come to see you."

He couldn't hear his father's reply, but while he waited for his sister, he leaned his forehead against Molly's.

"Right here with you, pal."

From behind, someone squeezed his shoulder.

Ella curled her hands around his arm.

Surrounded by the ones he loved most, in the home where he'd grown up and later been banished from, he was struck with profound sadness at the futility of it all. His father had lost one son tragically and had exiled another— and for what? It had all been such a terrible waste of energy.

"Linc?" Char said. "He'll see you now."

"You want me to wait out here?" Molly asked.

He tightened his grip on her hand so she couldn't get away. "Absolutely not."

Linc and Molly went into the room together, while the others waited in the hallway. Even though he'd known his once-robust father was seriously ill, seeing him sitting upright in a hospital bed, surrounded by oxygen tanks and beeping monitors, was still shocking. His dark hair was gone, replaced by thin whisps of white hair, and his mouth and nose were covered by an oxygen mask.

His father's eyes, however, were still sharp, even if they seemed sunken into his gaunt face. "Linc," he said. "You came."

"Hello, Father. You remember my wife, Molly?"

Carlton gave a nod to her before shifting his gaze back to Linc. "You look good."

"Thank you."

Carlton pulled at the oxygen mask.

Charlotte helped him remove it. "Just for a few minutes."

"Thank you for coming," he said to Linc, his voice soft and his breathing labored. "I wasn't sure if you would."

"I was raised to honor my father and mother."

"Even when they don't deserve it?"

"Even then."

A faint smiled played at the older man's lips. "I'm sorry. That's all I can say."

"Thank you for apologizing."

"I wish... I wish it hadn't happened."

"I do, too."

Char sniffled and dabbed at her eyes with a tissue.

"I brought some people I'd like you to meet," Linc said.

"He has *ten* children, Father."

Carlton's eyes went wide. "*Ten?*"

"That's right. Would you like to meet your grandchildren?"

"Yes, please. I'd like that very much."

While Linc went to get the others, Char replaced the oxygen mask on his face.

He introduced them all and mentioned the grandchildren who weren't with them.

Carlton pulled aside the mask. "You have a beautiful family."

"Thank you."

"Tell me…" Carlton took a breath. "Tell me about them."

"They all work in one way or another for the family businesses. Hunter, who's married to Megan, is the CFO of all our businesses, including the diner his wife, Megan, runs. Megan is also an amazing writer who's working on her first novel. Hannah was married to Caleb, but we lost him in Iraq. She's remarried to Nolan, who owns the auto repair garage in our town, and she makes beautiful jewelry that we sell in the store. Their daughter Callie's full name is Caleb, and she's going to be a big sister in the new year. Will oversees our Vermont Made line and is married to Cameron. Chase is his son. Ella is engaged to Gavin."

Gavin raised his hand to wave.

"He's Caleb's brother and owns a logging outfit in our area. Ella oversees the sales team in the store, among many other things. Charley, who lives with Tyler, is in charge of the inventory systems and all things technical, and Tyler is a very successful day trader and investor. Wade is our fitness and health guru. He oversees our wellness line, and his wife, Mia, works at the warehouse overseeing shipping and fulfillment. Colton manages our maple syrup operation with Max's help. Colton's wife, Lucy, is our webmaster along with Will's wife, Cameron."

Carlton seemed to be committing each detail to memory as Lincoln filled him in.

"Lucas and Landon are both lieutenants in the Butler Volunteer Fire Department. Lucas, who's engaged to Dani, is a master woodworker, and he sells his creations in the store. Dani, who's Savannah's mom, runs our warehouse. Landon is in charge of the family Christmas tree farm with Max's help. Landon is engaged to Amanda, who's Stella's mom. Amanda is in charge of our new catalog. Max is our youngest, but he was the first to make us grandparents with Caden, who turned one in November. He's an awesome single dad to his son, and we're super proud of him. We're proud of all of them." Linc gestured to Elmer to come closer. "This is my father-in-law, Elmer Stillman. His parents founded the business he entrusted to me when he retired."

Elmer looked directly at Carlton when he said, "Your son is an incredible businessman and an even more incredible husband, father, grandfather and uncle. I'm proud to call him my son-in-law and one of my closest friends."

Elmer's sweet words brought Linc's emotions surging to the surface.

"Thank you all for coming," Carlton said in a gruff whisper. "Thank you so much."

"We'll leave you to visit with your father, Dad," Hunter said, ushering the others out of the room.

"Impressive family," Carlton said.

"Thank you."

"The two boys… They're twins?"

"Yes, Lucas and Landon are identical twins. Hunter and Hannah, our eldest two, are also twins."

His father's eyes filled with tears. "Wish I had known them, that your mother had…"

"I wish that, too."

"Sorry, Lincoln," Carlton said as his eyes filled again. "So sorry."

"I have a question I need to ask, and it may not be the right time…"

His father waved his hand. "You can ask. There's not much time left."

"*Why*, Father? Why did you force me to choose between you and the woman I loved?"

Carlton closed his eyes, and when he did, tears leaked

from the corners. "When your brother died…" He opened his eyes and seemed to struggle for air. "That broke something in me. I was so angry at God and the world for taking him. He and I… We had a plan, and when he died…" He looked up at Linc. "I shouldn't have tried to force you to take his place. That wasn't fair to you."

"No one could replace him," Linc said softly.

"No, and I only compounded the tragedy by forcing you into an impossible position. I'm sorry for that and for keeping you from the others." He gave himself a minute to breathe. "I was just so damned *angry* for years after Hunter died, and by the time I snapped out of it… Well, the damage had certainly been done." He took a labored deep breath and looked up at Linc. "I wouldn't dare ask you to forgive me, but I hope, maybe, as a father yourself that you can understand what losing him did to me."

"I can't imagine losing a child, and I hope I never find out what that's like. I do forgive you, Father. It was a very long time ago, and I've moved on."

"That's generous of you. I hope you and the others can…"

"Already done." Lincoln looked across the bed at Charlotte. "We'll never be out of touch with each other again. I promise you that."

"That gives me peace, Linc. You've given me peace by coming all this way to see me." Carlton raised his hand.

Linc took his father's hand and gave it a squeeze.

"Tell me more about your life in Vermont."

For the next hour, Lincoln and Molly told him about the run-down barn they'd renovated into a showplace, about the store that had been at the center of their lives and the town moose named Fred, who was such a big part of the Butler, Vermont, community.

Carlton laughed at the story of Fred strolling through the

tent at Will and Cameron's wedding and then coming "home" with baby Dex.

"He's basically living in Hannah and Nolan's house," Molly said.

"She has an actual moose living in her house?"

"You'd have to know Hannah to fully understand why that's not even surprising," Linc said. "Her husband, Nolan, is a saint."

Carlton's eyes filled again. "I'm so sorry I don't know her. That I won't know her or the others. Tell me more about each of them."

Once again, Lincoln went through the list of his kids, filling his dad in on things about them that a grandparent would normally know by heart—awards, degrees, sports played and victories achieved. "Will was a champion-level skier. We thought he might make the Olympic team until he blew out his knee and ended his career. He went through a tough time after that, redefining himself, but he's bounced back and has found a wonderful life with Cameron and baby Chase."

Carlton hung on Lincoln's every word until a coughing fit seemed to deplete the last of his strength.

"Rest," Char said, patting their father's shoulder.

"Thank you, Lincoln," Carlton said without opening his eyes. "And Molly. Thank you both for coming and for bringing your beautiful family."

Lincoln leaned over and kissed his father's forehead. "Rest easy, Father."

Blinking back tears, he followed Char and Molly from the room. For a full minute, they only stood together, each of them seeming to process what'd just transpired. And then Charlotte broke the silence. "You truly gave him peace just now, Lincoln. Even if he didn't deserve it—"

"Everyone deserves peace in their final hours. I'm glad I was able to do that for him and that I could reconnect with you, Max and Will. That's what matters now. Where we go from here."

She nodded. "Yes, all we have is right now, and I want you back in my life. I want to know your children and have you know mine."

Linc stepped forward to hug his sister. "We'll make that happen."

A shout from downstairs had them breaking apart and heading for the stairs.

Colton was on his way up. "Ella's water broke."

SARAH STILLMAN GUTHRIE WAS BORN IN PHILADELPHIA AT three o'clock the next morning. Her exhausted grandparents and great-grandfather were on hand to help her elated parents welcome her into the world.

Elmer cried when he heard the baby's name. "Thank you for honoring my Sarah this way, sweetheart," he said as he kissed his granddaughter's forehead.

"She was one of my favorite people in the whole world," Ella said.

"Mine, too," Elmer said.

Gavin called his parents at home in Butler to share the happy news with them.

Leaving the new family to rest, Linc, Molly and Elmer took an Uber back to the hotel, where the others were spending a second, unexpected night.

"What a day—or two days, I should say—this has been," Linc said.

"Indeed." Elmer shook his head in disbelief. "You just never know what's going to happen next in this family."

"Thank God Gavin came on the trip," Molly said.

"That was a good call," Linc agreed.

They dropped Elmer off at the room he was again sharing with Charley and headed for their own room, using new keys that Hunter had brought to them at the hospital earlier. The delay in departure would get them home on Christmas Eve. They were hoping Ella and Gavin could come with them, but that hadn't been decided yet.

Linc hadn't been this exhausted in a very long time, and as Molly curled up to him in bed, he tried to come down from the emotionally charged day and night.

"How're you feeling?" Molly asked.

"Tired, wound up, drained…"

"We hardly got a chance to talk about the things your father said."

"It was nice to hear him say he was sorry it'd happened."

"I'm sure."

"And to see Char and the boys, who aren't boys anymore, and to hear I have nine nieces and nephews."

"It's all so painfully sad."

"It is," he said with a sigh. "And so unnecessary."

"Are you able to forgive him?" Molly asked.

"That's a complicated question. I can forgive him for being human, grieving his lost son and making mistakes that harmed a lot of people. However, I never saw my mother again, and he took actual steps to prevent me from contacting my siblings… Those are tougher things to forgive."

"You'd be a bigger person than I am if you could forgive him for either of those things."

"I'm glad I had the chance to see him one last time and to hear him express regret. That helps me cope with the rest of it."

"I hope so. We'll come back to see Char, Max and Will

and meet their families after the holidays. And we'll invite them to visit us, too."

"That'd be nice. I'd like that."

"Char said her daughter has an infant car seat they don't need any more that she's going to give Ella to get baby Sarah home to Vermont."

"Poor Ella, having to ride on a bus for seven hours after giving birth."

"If they decide to come with us, we can make her comfortable, and at least she'll have lots of help with the baby."

"True."

Lincoln yawned, and the next thing he knew, sunlight was streaming into the room. He glanced at the bedside clock and saw that it was eight thirty. "Hey, Mol."

She moaned.

"The kids are going to want to get going home."

She moaned again.

Laughing, he said, "Wake up, Granny. It's time to go home for Christmas."

"Christmas is canceled this year."

"No way. You'll have a riot on your hands."

They dragged themselves out of bed, showered, got dressed and joined the others for breakfast.

"How's Ella?" Charley asked after they shared the news of the delivery.

"Doing wonderfully," Molly replied. "Baby Sarah was eight pounds, six ounces, and twenty inches. Baby and Mom were resting comfortably when we left them early this morning."

"That's a relief," Charley said. "Will they be coming home with us?"

"We're going to check in with them this morning to see

what they want to do," Molly said. "How's everyone at home?"

"All good," Hunter said. "But I'm anxious to get home to Megan."

"Same," Colton said. "Lucy."

Having Ella go into labor early had the other expectant fathers on edge.

"We'll get you there as soon as we can," Linc said.

CHAPTER EIGHTEEN

"Count your age by friends, not years.
Count your life by smiles, not tears."
—John Lennon

*A*fter breakfast, they called the hospital to speak to Ella, who was also eager to get home. She and the baby were due to be released around eleven. "We'll be there," Linc told her.

"One of the nurses said Sarah is their first baby to go home on a bus full of relatives," Ella said.

"That's funny. Are you feeling up to the trip, honey?"

"I'll be fine. I just want to be home."

"We'll see you soon."

Linc ended the call and reported to the others about the timeline. Then he called Char to let her know they'd take her up on the offer of a car seat.

"I'll be there at eleven," Char said. "And congratulations on the new granddaughter, Linc."

"Thank you so much. We're thrilled for them."

~

ELLA AND GAVIN COULDN'T STOP STARING AT THEIR TINY princess, who had a light dusting of the dark hair she shared with both her parents.

"Do all new parents stare at their babies like crazy stalkers?" Ella asked him.

"I hope so, otherwise we're extra-crazy stalkers. I can't believe how pretty she is, although I should've known she would be. Check out her mom."

"And her dad. Handsomest guy in the whole wide world."

"If you say so."

"I say so."

"Is it super weird to say I see a hint of Caleb in her? Or is that just wishful thinking?"

"No, I see it, too. It's that little twisty thing she does with her lips. That's all him."

"It is, isn't it?"

Ella glanced at him and watched as he swiped at a tear.

"I hate that he'll never know her, that she'll never know him."

"She'll know him, Gav. She'll know him through us and through Hannah and your parents. He'll be part of her life. I promise."

He nodded and ran a finger over the baby's cheek. "She's so freaking perfect. Thank you for her."

"Thank *you* for her."

"You did all the hard work."

Ella leaned into him. "I couldn't have done it without you." She continued to gaze at the sleeping baby. "I've dreamed of her for years, and you made my dream come true. All my dreams have come true because of you. As long as I have you and Sarah, I have everything I need."

He held her close and kissed the top of her head. "You've got us, love."

~

THE BUS FULL OF ABBOTTS PULLED UP TO THE HOSPITAL'S MAIN entrance shortly before eleven. Linc and Molly got off the bus to go inside to help Ella and Gavin. Char was there with the car seat, and the baby was loaded up. Linc took the base of the seat to the bus and asked Lucas to install it for his sister. As firefighters, he and Landon were car seat experts.

When they were ready, Ella was rolled outside in a wheelchair while Gavin followed, carrying the baby in the seat. As they prepared to get on the bus, Ella's siblings gave her a round of applause.

"Way to go, Mama," Lucas said, hanging with his brothers from the open windows.

"Holy hot brothers," one of the nurses said to Ella.

"They're jackasses."

"They're *adorable*," the nurse said, laughing at their antics.

Linc hugged Char. "I'll be in touch."

"I'll look forward to hearing from you."

"Merry Christmas."

"Same to you, Linc. It was so great to see you and to meet your beautiful family."

"I can't wait to meet yours."

"We'll make that happen very soon."

They hugged once more, as if they were afraid they might not see each other again.

When everyone else was back on the bus, he left Char standing on the curb and waved to her as the bus pulled away.

"You'll see her soon," Molly said when he was seated with her.

"I really hope so."

"You will."

When they were on their way, Linc stood and turned to face the others. "I just want to say thanks to all of you for coming with me and supporting me through these last few days. And I want to thank you, Hunter, for handling the logistics and realizing that having you all in the room would make a much bigger statement than me telling my father I have ten children."

"We do tend to make a statement," Colton said, making everyone laugh.

"That's what happens when you're raised in a barn," the group of them said together.

Lincoln laughed at the familiar refrain. "Indeed." He glanced at Molly. "And now I want to tell you another story, this one about your mother."

Molly's brows furrowed with confusion. "What'd I do now?"

"It's what you did forty years ago, after the first time we were here together, that I want tell them."

"*Oh,*" she said, smiling as she tuned in to where he was going.

"When we got back to Vermont, we were still pretty shell-shocked by what'd happened with my father. We told your grandparents, and they were equally astounded. And then your mom, she went to her dad and told him I needed to know I still had a family. I had *their* family. She asked him to marry us that night."

"Whoa," Hannah said. "Did you do it, Gramps?"

"By then, I knew there was no coming between your parents, so of course I agreed."

"What did you say, Dad?" Lucas asked.

He looked down at the love of his life and reached for her hand. "When Molly Stillman got down on her knees and asked me to spend the rest of my life with her, starting that night, I said, 'Hell yes.' And your grandfather married us right there in their living room, three months before our official wedding."

"How have we never heard this?" Will asked.

"If I told you that, I would've had to tell you the rest, and I didn't want to talk about that. I didn't want you to know I was estranged from my family when I was raising you to be all about your family. I didn't want to set that example for you."

"It wasn't your fault you were estranged from them," Wade said.

"Still... I didn't want you to know something like that could happen, so we agreed to keep the first wedding between us and your grandparents. Megan overheard Elmer and me talking about it at the diner the other day, and she told me I needed to tell the rest of you about our first wedding so you'd know just how amazing your mother truly is."

"We already knew that," Hannah said. "But way to go, Mom." She led a rousing round of applause for Molly.

"Stand up and take a bow, love," Linc said.

Molly stood and bowed dramatically.

"And now you know all our secrets," Linc said.

"Not *all* of them," Molly reminded him. "There was that time—"

"*No,*" their children shouted.

Lincoln returned to his seat next to Molly.

"Thank you for the shout-out."

"My pleasure. Still ranks as one of your finest moments."

"I remember everything about that day so vividly. I was running on pure emotion and a ferocious need to do *something* to make things right for you. Not that I ever really could."

He leaned his head against hers. "You did, though. You fixed almost everything with that one gesture."

The family was in high spirits as they made their way north with Christmas music playing on the sound system. They even sang along, loudly and off-key, and the baby slept through the chaos.

"That makes her an official Abbott," Molly declared. "The ability to sleep through madness."

Lincoln had never seen Ella glow the way she did when she looked at her newborn daughter, and Gavin… He was an emotional disaster on his first day as a dad. The poor guy had been through so much since losing his beloved brother. To see him starting his own family with Ella was deeply satisfying to everyone who loved him.

"Your folks must be on pins and needles," Linc said to Gavin.

"They can't wait to meet her," Gav said, his gaze fixed on his fiancée and daughter. "They're so excited."

Bob and Amelia Guthrie had been part of the Abbott family for a long time, since Hannah married Caleb and made them family.

With rest stops and food breaks figured in, it took seven hours to reach the Vermont border, and a cheer went up inside the bus when they crossed the state line as a light snow fell.

"Ugh," Molly said. "I hope the snow doesn't slow us down."

"It might," Linc replied, leaning around her to see the snow coming down at a good clip. It was apt to be more significant in the mountains.

Sure enough, the closer they got to home, the slower they had to go to navigate snowy, icy roads.

"Should we stop somewhere?" Molly asked Linc in a soft tone that ensured they wouldn't be overheard.

"The kids would probably walk to get home if they had to, and knowing our kids, they'd do it."

"They get that from your people."

"No way," Linc said, smiling. "My people are refined city folk who know enough to stay inside when it's cold. Yours are the mountain people who think it's fun to go looking for people in a blizzard."

"For the record," she said, "that was never me. My father and his brothers and cousins, my brothers, yes. But never me."

"It's in your bloodline."

The friendly bickering helped to keep their minds off the increasingly hazardous weather conditions.

Caden was crying to be let out of his car seat, but Max told him he had to stay put for a little while longer.

Right before they would've lost reception in the mountains, Max's cell phone rang. "It's Cam. Hey, what's up?" After listening for a minute, he said, "Sure, I'll tell them. See you soon." After he ended the call, Max said, "Cameron and the others are at the barn waiting for us. She said they've set up beds for everyone, including you, Gramps, and have Christmas ready to go. They even have a bassinette for baby Sarah. They thought we'd want to be together this year."

"That's so wonderful," Molly said.

"They've been busy while we were gone," Linc said, touched by the efforts the others had gone to in their absence.

"They were busy making sure you're going to wake up to Christmas morning with your entire family," Molly said. "How amazing is that?"

"I can't imagine anything better."

~

WHAT SHOULD'VE BEEN A TWENTY-MINUTE RIDE TOOK TWO
hours in the snow as the bus crept toward home on slick
mountain roads. The usually boisterous group was mostly
silent as the tension grew. They were used to driving in
snow, even blizzards. But they drove four-wheel-drive vehi-
cles designed to navigate mountain roads in the snow. The
bus was not equipped for this weather.

"Are you sure we shouldn't pull off the road?" Molly
asked Linc.

"We probably should, but where would we go? Everything is closed, and there's not a hotel for miles." Linc
wrapped both his hands around hers. "It'll be okay, honey.
Bill's the best. He'll get us home safely." He said what she
needed to hear, but his anxiety spiked. Being stranded in a
blizzard wasn't an option, especially with a newborn and two
other little ones with them.

Linc didn't breathe easily until they reached the outer
limits of Butler a half hour later. "Home sweet home," he said
to a visibly relieved Molly.

"Thank goodness."

"Hey, Bill, watch out for a welcoming committee in the
form of a very large moose who likes to stand in the middle
of the road."

"On the lookout," Bill replied.

Linc directed him through town, over the single-lane
covered bridge and to the righthand turn that took them
onto Hells Peak Road. Finally. Nearly ten hours after they'd
left Philly, they were home. Every light was on in the barn, or
so it seemed, and the outdoor holiday lights were
illuminated.

"I've never been so happy to see our formerly falling-
down barn where cows used to live," Molly said.

"Me either."

Everyone thanked Bill for getting them home safely as they got off the bus and trooped into the warm, welcoming barn where the rest of their loved ones waited.

"Will you be all right getting home, Bill?" Linc asked.

"Sure thing. I only have to go to St. Johnsbury to drop the bus and pick up my car, and then it's a short way home from there."

Linc shook his hand. "Thank you again for sacrificing Christmas Eve with your family to drive mine."

"It was a pleasure, Linc. Merry Christmas to you and yours."

"Same to you."

When Linc stepped off the bus, George and Ringo danced around in the driving snow, barking with joy to have him home. As the last one in, Linc noticed coats hanging from every one of the ten hooks in the mudroom, and a feeling of profound peace came over him even as the sound of bedlam echoed through the big barn.

They were used to bedlam around there, so it was only fitting that this Christmas should be a throwback to years past.

In the kitchen, he encountered Hunter in a passionate embrace with Megan and continued past them to the dining room, where Hannah and Nolan were kissing around Callie, who wanted her daddy's undivided attention after a couple of days without him.

Wade walked by with Mia wrapped around him as he made for the stairs, and Colton had Lucy pressed up against the hallway wall while she giggled madly at something he was saying.

Linc stepped into the family room, where the massive ten-foot Christmas tree they got every year was the focal point, and a huge fire burned in the hearth. Will was on the floor with his arms around Cameron and baby Chase, who was asleep on his mother's chest. Stella was holding baby Savannah as Lucas reunited with Dani, and Landon hugged Amanda.

Ella was already on the sofa, covered with a blanket as she nursed Sarah with Gavin seated right beside her in case they needed anything.

"You don't have to stay if this is too much for you," Linc said to them.

Ella looked up at him, her dark eyes bright with joy. "We wouldn't miss this for anything. And Sarah needs to get used to the chaos she's been born into."

Linc bent to kiss his daughter's cheek. "It wouldn't be the same without your little family. Thank you for the gift of baby Sarah. She's the best Christmas present we could've hoped for."

Charley sat on Tyler's lap, his arms around her, her head on his chest, seeming relieved to be back with him.

Linc loved them together. Tyler's low-key personality was perfect for his delightfully complicated daughter.

"We have a ton of food ready," Cam told Linc. "Are you hungry?"

"I could eat something."

"We're ready for you," his daughter-in-law said with a warm smile. "And we all want to know how you're doing."

"I'm good. The trip went well. I made some peace with the past and came home with a new granddaughter to a house full of love. What more could I need?"

"We thought you might like to have everyone here this year," Cam said.

"You thought exactly right. I can't imagine anything better than this."

"They even brought all the cars home from the store," Will said. "They thought of everything."

"We didn't want you to have to think about anything

other than enjoying the holiday," Cam said. "It was the least we could do for the family that's done so much for us."

Linc squeezed her shoulder. "Thank you, sweetheart."

CHAPTER NINETEEN

"Reality leaves a lot to the imagination."
—John Lennon

*W*ade carried Mia into the former linen closet that he'd turned into a bedroom for himself so he could escape the madness of life in the barn when he'd still lived at home. He kicked the door closed behind them, put her down on the narrow twin bed and returned to the door to lock it, leaving nothing to chance after being without his love for six endless days.

He stretched out next to her and brought her in for another sweet kiss. "We're never doing this again."

"Doing what?"

"Spending six days apart."

"It was brutal. I wandered around aimlessly from the time I got home until Cameron called to tell me the plan to get Christmas ready here."

"That was a really nice thing you all did for my dad."

"It was all her idea, and selfishly, I was glad to have something to do other than go crazy from missing you."

"I'm secretly glad that you felt as crazy as I did."

"It was bad. What does that say about us?"

"That we know a good thing when we've got it." He wrapped his arms around her and held on tight. "I can't believe it's already been almost a year since you showed up half frozen on my doorstep and asked me to marry you."

"Best thing I ever did."

"Best thing *I* ever did was say yes to you."

Their kisses became more desperate as they pulled at clothes until they were naked and he hovered above her, dying for her.

She reached for him, wrapped her arms and legs around him and sighed with pleasure as he joined their bodies.

"*Yes,*" he whispered against her neck. "That's what I needed."

"Me, too. I can't remember how I ever lived without you."

They rarely talked anymore about the years they'd spent aching for each other, but the reminder of what they'd been through never failed to stir deep feelings of gratitude for what they had now.

"It was pure torture, knowing you were out there but so far out of reach."

She hugged him close to her, surrounding him in the kind of love he'd never dreamed possible until he'd found her.

They moved together like a well-choreographed dance team, their bodies straining for the release they craved until it rolled over them in waves of pleasure so intense, it took his breath away.

"Welcome home," she said with a giggle that made him smile.

"Best welcome-home I've ever gotten."

~

"SHE SHOULD BE IN BED," NOLAN SAID OF CALLIE, WHO WAS running around with Caden, the two of them acting like they'd been shot full of jet fuel.

"We need to let them burn some energy from being cooped up all day," Hannah said, "or they'll never sleep."

They sat on the floor in front of the fire, keeping an eye on their daughter and her cousin, who weren't showing any signs of winding down.

Homer Junior was curled up on Hannah's lap, as relieved to have her home as Nolan was.

Nolan put his arm around Hannah and brought her in closer to him. "My baby mama needs some rest. You look tired."

"I know! I hate that."

Nolan kissed both her cheeks. "You're beautiful, but I don't want you getting run down."

She rested her head on his shoulder, thankful to be back with him in time for Christmas. For a while there, she'd worried they wouldn't be able to get home in the storm. "How's my baby Dexter?"

"He's been a sad sack without you, just like me, Fred and Homie. I tried to tell them we should enjoy our rare boys-only time, but they weren't having it."

"Is Dude taking care of him while we're here?"

"Yep. Skeeter said not to worry about a thing. They'd take the snowmobiles over to feed him and let him out. I told Skeeter if I find giant piles of moose poop in my house, he's fired."

Hannah giggled at that. "He'd never poop in my house."

"He'd better not, or he's gone."

"Stop it. You know you love him as much as I do."

"I do not. My problem is that I love *you* enough to let you convince me to allow a wild animal to live in our home."

"He's not a wild animal. He's our little boy."

"You're off your rocker, as always."

"That's how you like me."

"Wouldn't have you any other way, but the moose poop is a deal breaker."

"That's good to know," she said, yawning.

"Linc, would you please watch our wild child while I put the moose whisperer to bed?" Nolan asked.

"Yep, I've got her."

"I'm here, too," Max said.

"Be right back," Nolan said as he helped Hannah up and led her toward the stairs, where he steered her up with his hands on her hips.

Hannah was so tired, she offered no resistance. "You'll get Callie to bed?"

"I'll take care of her. Don't worry."

"K."

Nolan helped her change into the flannel pajamas she preferred in the winter and even went so far as to put toothpaste on her toothbrush for her before walking her back into their room and tucking her in under a down comforter.

It was all she could do to keep her eyes open long enough to kiss him good night. "Sorry to be so sleepy."

"Don't be sorry."

"Missed you so much when we were gone."

"Missed you like crazy. The boys and I agreed that nothing is fun without our girls." He kissed her and leaned his forehead against hers. "Get some sleep, sweetheart."

"Want to snuggle with you."

"We'll do that tomorrow."

"Promise?"

"Promise."

Hannah fell asleep with a smile on her face.

~

"I CAN'T BELIEVE YOU ORGANIZED THIS FOR US," WILL SAID TO
Cameron, who had Chase sleeping in her arms.

"I thought your dad might enjoy having everyone
together for Christmas."

"You thought right, and I just want to point out that as
someone who grew up as an only child, you've completely
conquered the big-family dynamic."

"You really think so?"

"Hell yes. We all think so. Look at what you did here,
babe. You found a way for all of us to spend Christmas Eve
together."

"Thanks," she said, seeming pleased by the praise.

The glow of the firelight on her pretty face made him
want her so fiercely. Speaking close to her ear, he said, "Let's
go to bed."

"I'm ready."

He took Chase from her, held him with one arm and
reached for her with his free hand to help her up. "We'll see
you in the morning," Will said to the others as he took his
family to bed.

"Sleep well, guys," Linc said. "And, Cam… Thank you
again."

"My pleasure."

With his hand on her lower back, Will guided his wife to
the stairs and followed her up. He settled Chase in the
portable crib in the corner, swept his fingers over the baby's
soft blond hair and left him to sleep, knowing he'd be up
early.

Will stripped down to boxers and crawled into bed with
Cameron, so relieved to be back with her and Chase. "That
ride home was nerve-racking. I was so afraid we weren't
going to get here for Christmas."

"We were so worried. We had a lot of loved ones on that bus."

He released a deep sigh and then inhaled the distinctive scent of his love. "I missed you and Chase so much."

"We missed you, too. It was only two nights, but it felt like two weeks."

"I know. We all said that. I'm really glad we went, but I'm super glad to be home."

"Your dad seems good."

"He does. I think it gave him some peace of mind to have his dad tell him he was wrong to do what he did and that he regrets it."

"That must've been nice to hear."

"I'm sure it was, but it's just so freaking sad and pointless when you really think about it."

"I was thinking about it while you were gone, and I wonder if losing his older son did something to him, made him desperate to hold on to the others or something."

"From what Dad said, that's pretty much what happened. Who knows what that kind of loss does to people?"

She shuddered. "God, I hope we never find out."

"Me, too."

After a pause, she said, "You know, I saw it in my own dad, how much my mother's sudden death affected him and how he raised me at arm's length, almost as if he was afraid to care too much about me out of fear he could lose me, too. Grief does strange things to people."

"You're right. It does for sure. I suppose all that matters is that my dad and his father had the chance to make peace before he dies."

"Your dad is better off for having done that. I really believe that."

"Speaking of dads, yours is still coming this week, right?"

"Yep. They're in Florida with Mary's parents for Christmas and coming here for New Year's."

"That's good. I'm looking forward to seeing them."

"I am, too. He won't believe how big Chase has gotten since they were here in October." She yawned and snuggled into his chest. "I'm so tired."

"Pulling off Christmas for twenty-six people is exhausting."

"I had a ton of help, and it's going to be closer to forty. Gavin's parents, Dani's parents, Hannah and Ray are coming tomorrow, and so are Gray, Emma and Simone. We also invited Dude, Skeeter and Mildred to come for dinner."

"This barn is gonna rock this Christmas."

"It sure is. I can't wait. The sitcom families I used to watch growing up had nothing on the Abbotts."

"The Abbotts are better for having Cameron Murphy around, especially this Abbott. I love you so much."

"Love you, too."

"HOW SOON CAN WE GO TO BED?" LANDON ASKED AMANDA, his lips close to her ear so he couldn't be overheard.

"Not until Stella does."

"When will that be?"

She turned to look at him, seated behind her on a chaise. "What's your hurry, cowboy?"

He pulled her back against him, pressing his erection against her back. "Any questions?"

"Ah, so it's like that, is it?"

"Whenever you're around."

"I'm around a lot. That must get painful."

He grunted out a laugh. "Sure does, especially after spending two endless nights without you."

"You're kind of being pathetic right now."

"I can't help it if I love you so much that being away from you was painful."

"I love you, too, and I missed you just as much. Stella kept saying it was wicked quiet without you around."

"I'm not sure if I should be complimented or insulted by that."

"Probably a little of both."

"Look at her," he said of Stella, who was stretched out on the floor reading a book to Savannah, Caden and Callie. "She's so good with them."

"They adore her. The minute she comes into the room, the three of them are all over her."

"We ought to get busy giving her some siblings," he said.

"You think so?"

"Absolutely. She'll be the best big sister ever."

"She will."

He pressed against her again. "How about we start now?"

Amanda giggled. "Stop it. You're in a room full of relatives, making a scene."

"They're used to me making scenes, and they don't know what we're talking about."

"I bet they could guess."

"Look at Luc over there with Dani. I'll bet the farm that he's trying to talk her into going to bed for the same reason I want you in my bed."

"You're embarrassing me, Landon."

"I can live with that, Amanda. So, bed. Now. Yes? Stella can tuck herself in this one time. She's a big girl."

"I'm not going to miss tucking her in on our first Christmas Eve together."

Landon groaned dramatically. "It's our first Christmas Eve together, too. Are you going to miss tucking me in?"

"I'll tuck you in *after* I tuck her in."

"Now you're just being mean to me."

She lost it laughing, which only made him want her more. He'd never pictured himself being in love with anyone the way he was with her.

When Stella finished the story she was reading to the kids, their parents scooped them up to take them up to bed.

"Thank you, Jesus," Landon said. "Meet me in bed after you tuck in our girl."

"Go warm it up for me."

Landon held out his arms to hug and kiss Stella good night. They'd already read *'Twas the Night Before Christmas* as a group and put out cookies for Santa that they'd had to protect from the many dogs in residence that night.

"Glad you made it home for Christmas, Landon," Stella said with a smile.

"Me, too, sweetheart. See you in the morning."

Amanda got up to go with Stella to get her and Matilda settled on the sofa in his dad's home office.

Landon had worried that Stella might be scared sleeping by herself in there, but she'd told them that she'd be fine as long as Matilda was there. He was just glad they weren't sharing a room with her so they could have some time alone. As it was, he had to wait a good ten minutes after Amanda walked away before he could get up and leave the room without embarrassing himself.

"Going to bed?" Lucas asked.

"Yep."

"Right behind you, brother. I'm bushed."

"Merry Christmas."

"Same to you."

Landon stepped over Colton and Lucy, who seemed to be inclined to sleep right there in the middle of the family room, and headed for one of the four first-floor bedrooms that'd been assigned to him and Amanda.

Getting to Christmas Eve was always a huge relief to him, having survived another wildly busy season at the tree farm. He gave himself a couple of weeks off from the place before getting back to work there in mid-January. And knowing he had two more days off before he had to be back to work at the firehouse helped to put him in a festive mood.

After stripping off his clothes, he sat on the bed to test whether it was squeaky and was relieved to discover it wasn't. That was good news indeed.

He was lying on the bed, naked as the day he was born, when Amanda came in a few minutes later.

"Oh, for crying out loud, Landon. What if someone else had come in here by mistake?"

"They would've gotten one hell of a show."

She rolled her eyes. "You're a little full of yourself."

He curled a hand around his erection. "I don't hear you complaining about what I've got going on."

"You're like a middle school boy."

"Duh, you've known that since the day you met me. Now get over here and put me out of my middle school misery."

She made a show out of removing her clothes as slowly and seductively as she possibly could.

Watching her reveal herself to him, he could only marvel at how lucky he was that such a beautiful, sweet, smart, special woman loved him the way she did. And then she locked the door, crawled onto the bed and straddled him, making him feel like he'd died and gone straight to heaven. "Now that's what I'm talking about."

"It's what you're always talking about."

"That's your fault."

She raised a brow to call him out on his bullshit, which was one of her many special gifts. "How so?"

He reached up to cup her breasts and ran his thumbs over

hard nipples. "You're so sexy, you make me want you all the time."

"And that's my fault?"

"Yep."

"Good to know."

"I joke around a lot with you, but you know how much I love you, right?"

"Yes, Landon, I know that, and I love that you joke around with me all the time. You're very good for my ego."

"Your ego should be very, very healthy. The one thing I'd never joke about is how much I love you, how much I want you and how much better everything is now that I have you and Stella and Matilda in my life."

"I love our little family. It's the best thing to ever happen to me. You're the best thing. You and Stella…"

He reached for her and brought her down to him for a deep, sexy kiss that had him on the verge of begging her to put him out of his misery. Fortunately, he never had to beg. She knew what he needed and was almost always happy to give it to him.

She raised herself up and came down on him, taking his cock into her tight, wet heat in a slow, sexy slide that had his eyes rolling back in his head.

"Fuck me, that's so good," he whispered.

"I am fucking you," she said with a teasing smile, moving like the sexiest seductress he'd ever seen as she rode him.

"Shit, this is gonna be fast, which is also your fault."

"How so?"

"You've had me primed for hours."

"Again I ask, how so?"

"By breathing."

She tweaked his nipples and made him jolt. "You're ridiculous."

"Only with you. I've never wanted anyone the way I want

you. All you have to do is walk in the door, and I'm ready to go."

"Oh, lucky me!"

"You're *so* lucky."

She laughed and bent to kiss him. "So very lucky indeed."

CHAPTER TWENTY

"Close your eyes and I'll kiss you. Tomorrow I'll miss you."
—Paul McCartney

ucas followed Dani into the room where they were sleeping with Savannah and hoped it wasn't too much to ask that she'd go down easy so he could have some time alone with his love.

"She's on fire tonight," Dani said. "I can't believe she's still going with no nap today."

The minute Dani put her on the bed, Savannah popped up to start jumping.

Lucas nabbed her out of the air. "Time to settle down, sweet girl. Santa can't come if little girls are still awake."

"Santa, Lu."

"That's right, baby girl. If you want Santa to come, you have to go night-night."

"No, Lu."

"Yes, Savvy."

"No, Lu."

Dani covered her mouth to contain the laughter that was

trying to get out. After Lu, her nickname for Lucas, *no* had become their little girl's second-favorite word. She hadn't even said Mama yet, but she had *no* fully mastered.

"Do not laugh," he said to Dani.

"Trying so hard."

Lucas walked her around the room for thirty minutes until she began to surrender to sleep. He rubbed her back and whispered to her about sweet dreams and sugar plums and Santa coming on his sleigh to bring good girls lots of presents. All the while, he thought about what he'd been doing a year ago on Christmas Eve. After dinner with his family, he and Landon had gone barhopping with some friends from the firehouse.

How different both their lives were now, and he wouldn't go back to how it'd been for anything. Having Dani and Savvy in his life was the best thing to ever happen to him. In this coming year, he and Dani would get married and maybe add to their little family. He couldn't wait for everything they had ahead of them.

When he was sure that Savvy was asleep, he kissed her and put her down in the portable crib. Then he shook out his arms, which were tingling with pins and needles from holding her for so long.

"My hero," Dani whispered when he joined her in bed.

"I love her so freaking much."

"She loves you just as much. You've got the magic touch with her."

"Do I have it with you, too?" he asked, cupping her backside to bring her in closer to him.

"Always," she said, smothering a yawn. She'd been working seven days a week for two months at the warehouse and was off until after New Year's Day. He'd taken the week off, too, and couldn't wait to spend it with her.

He kissed her forehead and then her lips. "Get some sleep, love. You're exhausted."

Her eyes fluttered open. "You don't want to…"

"Always," he said, echoing her comment. "But you need sleep more than you need me tonight."

"I need you more," she said, yawning again.

"Sleep. We've got a whole week to snuggle."

"Mmm, can't wait."

"Me either."

~

"COLTON."

"Hmmm."

"*Colton.*"

He opened one eye to his favorite thing to look at—Lucy's adorable face.

"We need to go to bed."

"I can't move."

"You have to move, or your pregnant wife is going to sleep on the floor, which will make me cranky on Christmas. Do you want me cranky on Christmas?"

"Nope."

She poked his ribs, and he startled awake.

"Damn, woman."

"Take me to bed, Colton, or else."

Since he didn't want to find out what *or else* entailed, he forced himself to stand and to help her up, holding her for a second until she was steady. As she reached the last month of pregnancy, she lost her balance more often. "You good, babe?"

"I'll be better when I'm in a bed."

Their dogs, Sarah and Elmer, looked up to see where they were going, but decided to stay put next to the fire, where they were snuggled up to Tucker and Tanner as well as George, Ringo, Homer and Horace. There were nearly as many dogs in the house tonight as there were people.

Colton and Lucy said good night to his dad and grandfather, who were enjoying a nightcap before bed.

"Sleep well, children," Elmer said.

"I'll let the pups out one more time before I go to bed," Linc said.

"Thanks, Dad," Colton said. "Good night."

"Night, son."

"Are you feeling okay?" Colton asked Lucy when they were on the way upstairs.

"Other than being fat and my boobs aching, I'm just dandy."

"You're not fat. You're beautiful."

"I can be both."

"You're the most gorgeous pregnant woman I've ever seen."

"You have to say that. You did this to me."

"I did a rather spectacular job of knocking you up, didn't I?"

She turned to face him and squeezed his lips shut.

Colton, being Colton, kept talking anyway. "Admit it," he said, his voice muffled. "No one has ever knocked up anyone better than I knocked you up."

Lucy, being Lucy, knew just how to shut him up when she'd heard enough out of him. She curled her arms around his neck and kissed him.

That always worked to shut him up. Temporarily, anyway.

He picked her up to carry her the rest of the way up the stairs and eased her onto the bed, landing next to her, all without breaking the kiss that became more desperate by the second. "I thought you were tired."

"I am," she said, reaching for him.

Colton loved pregnant Lucy and how she couldn't get enough sex, no matter how often they did it. That worked for him.

"Hurry," she said.

He hurried, and when they came together in a moment of heat and need and love so big it threatened to consume him, he gave thanks as he often did for whatever stroke of fate had brought her to him. Making love with his Lucy was a nearly religious experience, every damned time, especially after having been away from her for three endless days and two long nights.

"Missed you so much," he whispered as he moved in her, careful not to put weight on the baby.

"Missed you, too. Our mountain isn't the same without my mountain man."

"I was worried about you up there by yourself."

"I wasn't by myself. Sarah and Elmer took good care of me."

Colton pushed into her and held still while grasping her hips, knowing how that drove her wild.

"Colton," she said, sounding desperate. "Don't torture me."

"Why not? I love to torture you."

She pinched his butt and made him startle, which got him moving again.

"That was a dirty trick, my love."

"Whatever it takes."

"Is this what you want?" he asked, picking up the pace.

"*Yes,*" she said, arching into him as best she could with the beach ball between them.

"Hold that thought," he said, withdrawing from her.

"Ugh."

He carefully arranged her on her knees and entered her from behind.

"Don't stop," she said.

"Shhh, we're not on the mountain."

"Do. Not. *Stop.*"

Colton laughed as he gave his love what she wanted, reminding her again to be quiet as they reached a highly satisfying conclusion.

"Was I loud?" Lucy asked as she melted into the bed.

Colton withdrew from her and turned on his side to face her. "Very, but that's fine. It's good for people to know how happy I keep you."

She squished his lips again, making him laugh. "You keep me very happy, but your ego is out of control."

"Just the way you like it."

"Whatever you say."

"I love you, my Lucy in the sky with diamonds, the best thing to ever happen to me."

"I love you, too, Colton, my mountain man with an ego bigger than the sun."

"We're a match made in heaven."

"If you say so."

"I do. I say so."

Since she was already most of the way asleep, he settled for having the last word.

HUNTER HAD TROUBLE WINDING DOWN FROM THE EMOTIONAL few days with his family, his mind racing with the things he'd learned about his father's past. He wanted to know more about the uncle he'd been named for and would ask his dad about him when things settled down.

Megan was downstairs seeing to some last-minute details

for breakfast, which she was in charge of. Breakfast for more than two dozen people would be nothing for her, but he was worried about her overdoing it. He was thinking about going after her when she came into the room.

"There you are. I was about to come fetch you."

"Breakfast is going to be *epic*."

"With you in charge, I have no doubt. Now come get in bed with your lonely husband who missed you so much."

"I'm coming."

When she snuggled up to him a few minutes later, he felt himself begin to relax. She was usually the fix for whatever ailed him. Why should now be any different?

"I could tell you were stressed when you got home," she said. "Are you better now?"

"Getting there." He held her close. "This helps."

"The trip went well, though, right?"

"Yeah, it was fine, all things considered. It just has me thinking a lot about how you don't really know people and what they've endured. Even the people closest to you sometimes."

"It's true. I see your dad every day. I have for years. And I had no idea any of this had happened to him."

"He didn't want us to know."

"He didn't want you to hurt for him."

"I suppose."

"And yet you have anyway, haven't you?"

"A little."

"You have the biggest heart, Hunter. It's one of the things I love the best about you."

Ready to lighten up his mood, he said, "What are some of the other things?"

"I love the way you take care of me and everyone else you love. I adore your gorgeous brown eyes and your handsome face and sexy body and—"

He kissed her, devouring her lips in a passionate kiss that wiped his mind clear of anything that wasn't her and them and how it felt to be with her this way. On many a day, even a year after their wedding, he still wanted to pinch himself to believe he'd actually gotten the woman of his dreams to marry him. "Happy anniversary," he said against her lips. "Best year of my life."

"Happy anniversary." She ran her fingers through his hair and gazed up at him with her heart in her eyes. "Best year of my life, too."

"I can't wait for year two."

"I'm looking forward to all the years."

"Mmm, me, too."

"How much sex do you think is happening in this barn tonight?" Charley asked Tyler.

"A lot."

"The elixir you injected me with before I left on the trip has worn off, and I have to spend all day tomorrow with my siblings. I think I need another infusion to ensure family unity on Christmas."

Tyler's low rumble of laughter made her smile. Three days and two nights without him had made her realize she was even more dependent upon his presence in her life than she'd previously believed. And that was saying something.

He turned so he hovered above her, looking down at her with the fierce, sexy look that let her know every day that she was the center of his universe. "I'm always happy to tame you, as long as you know I love you just the way you are."

"That's why I'm here. Because you get me."

"I get you, and getting you is the best thing to ever happen to me."

She reached for him, bringing him into her embrace. "Merry Christmas, Ty."

"Merry Christmas, Charl."

"IS SHE ASLEEP?" GAVIN ASKED WHEN ELLA FINISHED FEEDING baby Sarah.

"I think so."

"Should we put her in the bassinette?"

"Probably."

"You don't want to?"

Ella gazed down at the tiny face that had taken over her life in the span of twenty-four hours. "I want to hold her all the time."

"Didn't the books say we're not supposed to do that?"

"Yep."

"So…"

"I want to hold her all the time."

Gavin laughed and put his arm around her so he could hold her while she held the baby she'd wanted for so long. "Are you still hurting?"

"*So* bad, but it was worth it. She's perfect, isn't she?"

"Almost as perfect as her mommy." He kissed the top of Ella's head. "Now let's put her down so you can get some rest. She'll be awake again in a couple of hours."

"I can't wait."

Smiling, he got up, took the baby and settled her in the bassinette. "Are you sure she doesn't need a blanket?"

"No, the sleeper is her blanket. We don't want anything else in there with her."

He bent to kiss the baby's forehead. "Sleep tight, little one." Leaving her to sleep, he slid into bed with Ella and brought her head to rest on his chest. "Are you comfortable?"

"Uh-huh, but I just realized I never got to finish your Christmas present."

"Yes, you did. She's sleeping in her bassinette."

"I made something else for you, but it's not done."

"No worries, sweetheart. I'll still love it whenever you get a chance to finish it."

"How do you know that?"

"Because I love everything you've ever given me. You saved my life with your big love, my sweet Ella, and gave me the most beautiful little girl. You don't ever have to give me anything else again."

"I feel guilty."

"Why?"

"Because I'm this happy when so many other people aren't."

"Enjoy this moment you've waited so long to have. This, right here and now, is all there is."

Since he knew of what he spoke, she decided to take his wise advice.

CHAPTER TWENTY-ONE

"In the end, the love you take is equal to the love you make."
—Paul McCartney

 inc was about to call it a night when Max came
downstairs, poured himself a glass of the whiskey he
and Elmer had opened and sat with them in front of
the fire.

"Everything all right, son?"

"Sure, everything is great. I think all my siblings are
currently having sex while I'm sitting here with you two."
Max took a big sip of the whiskey. "But yeah, I'm good."

Elmer rubbed a hand over his mouth as if trying not to
laugh.

"You'll find your person, Max," Linc said. "I have no doubt
about that, and when you do, it'll be a love affair for the ages."

"Any time now."

"You're not ready yet," Elmer said.

"How's that?"

"You're only twenty-three."

"Mom wasn't even twenty-three when she married Dad."

"Touché," Elmer said. "You've got all the time in the world. Look at Hunter. He was thirty-five or -six when he settled down with Megan."

"I'm not waiting that long," Max said. "That's an eternity. I'm already sick of being alone."

"You're never alone in this family," Linc reminded him.

"And I'm incredibly grateful for that, but you know what I mean. I want what they have." He gestured randomly behind him, referring to his siblings, who were all in bed with their partners.

"You'll have it," Elmer said. "I have no doubt about that whatsoever. You, my dear boy, are meant for a great love."

"*When?*"

"When the time is right."

"How will I know when the time is right?"

"When you meet someone you can't live without. Until that happens, enjoy being single and have some fun."

"I have a one-year-old."

"And plenty of babysitters," Linc reminded him. "You never want to ask for help, but we're always willing to give it."

"Mom watches him all day while I work. That's the last thing she wants to do at night."

"Mom loves every second she spends with him, and so do I. If you hadn't asked her to watch him while you work, she would've offered. In case you haven't noticed, your mom loves kids."

"Still… I don't want to take advantage."

Elmer leaned in, elbows on his knees, his expression intense but loving. "Listen to what your dad is saying, Max. They like helping with Caden. They would say so if they didn't. So stop manufacturing issues that don't exist. Put your son to bed, leave your folks in charge and go out and have some fun. You're only going to be twenty-three once.

Enjoy your life. The time for serious and permanent will come. When it's the right person."

"You promise?"

"I promise, and I've never broken a promise to you yet, have I?"

"Nope."

"I'm not going to start now."

"Thanks, Gramps. You're the best."

"Aw, thanks, but you should know I'm not going anywhere until every one of you kids is happy and settled, so take your time. Keep your favorite old man around a little longer."

"I'll do that. In fact, I may never get married if that'll keep you here forever."

"Nah, don't do that. I want you to have what I had with my Sarah and what your dad has had with your mom, even if I wanted to kill him at first."

Linc rolled his eyes. "Don't listen to him. It was love at first sight between the two of us."

"Sure, it was," Elmer said, laughing. "The impertinence of him showing up holding my little girl's hand."

"The ridiculousness never ends around here."

Listening to them had Max laughing when only a few minutes ago, he'd been bummed out at the realization that he was once again alone in a sea of happy couples. Leave it to his dad and grandfather to snap him out of the funk.

"I'm off to bed," Max said after downing the last of his drink. He'd love to have another, but Caden would be up early, and he didn't need to be hungover on Christmas.

"Walk me up, my friend," Elmer said. "I've forgotten which room is mine, and I'm terribly afraid to walk into the wrong room up there and see something that can never be forgotten."

Linc and Max laughed.

"Probably a good idea," Linc said.

"Come on, Gramps. I'll get you settled with no trauma."

"Appreciate that. Linc, I'll see you in the morning."

"See you then. In the meantime, I'm going to snuggle with your daughter."

"Impertinent ass," Elmer muttered.

Max laughed. "That's just a rude thing to say to your father-in-law, Dad."

"I know. Why do you think I said it?"

"You see what I've had to deal with all these years, my boy?"

"I see, Gramps. It hasn't been easy being you with those two to deal with."

"Not easy at all."

~

LATE ON CHRISTMAS DAY, AFTER PRESENTS HAD BEEN exchanged and a ton of food consumed, Ella asked if she could have everyone's attention before they all went their separate ways.

"As long as I don't have to move, I'm all yours, El," Colton said from his post on the floor, stretched out next to the Christmas tree, Lucy leaning against him. The guys had spent two hours after dinner snow-blowing and digging their cars out so everyone could go home later.

"You don't have to move," Ella told him. "Gavin and I had planned a little surprise for today, not knowing we had our own little surprise about to arrive a couple of weeks early."

"What's your surprise?" Charley asked, smothering a yawn as she snuggled with Tyler on the sofa.

Ella looked to Elmer. "Gramps? Are you ready?"

"Ready, willing and able, my love," Elmer said as he pulled

himself up and joined Ella, who held baby Sarah, and Gavin in front of the fireplace.

"What's happening?" Molly asked.

"Just a little wedding," Ella said, smiling up at Gavin.

His mother, Amelia, let out a happy shout and hugged her husband, Bob, and then Molly and Linc. "Here we go again," Amelia said, beaming as another Guthrie prepared to marry another Abbott.

"We wanted to do it while everyone was together," Gavin said. "We had no idea we'd also have our daughter here."

"She just makes it perfect," Ella said, kissing her daughter's forehead.

"Are you two kids ready to say 'I do'?" Elmer asked.

"I am," Ella said, smiling at Gavin.

"Hell yes," Gavin said.

"Charley and Hannah, will you be my attendants?"

While she waited for her sisters to join her, Ella saw Amelia wiping tears.

Hannah hugged Ella, and then Charley did the same.

"Thanks for asking us," Hannah said for both of them.

"There's no one else I would've asked."

"Will and Hunter," Gavin said, "we've been friends for as long as I can remember, and since my own brother can't be here to stand up for me, I'd appreciate if you guys would."

Hunter put his hand on his heart as he stood to join Will and Gavin. "Honored, brother," he said when he hugged Gavin.

"What he said," Will added.

Ella couldn't help but note that her handsome, smiling groom bore no resemblance whatsoever to the devastated shell of a man he'd been a few years ago. Their life together had helped to put his pieces back together, and while he'd never be the same person he'd been before he lost his brother, he was a new, stronger version of that person, and Ella loved him with her whole heart and soul.

"Ella and Gavin wanted to write their own vows, so I'm only here to tell them what to do and when to do it," Elmer said, beaming. "Ladies first. Ella?"

She handed the baby to her mother so she could focus exclusively on the love of her life. "I'd bought a dress and was going to do something with my hair, but then Sarah arrived and it snowed and here we are, in sweats and flannels at our wedding, and somehow that's exactly how it should be. I'm never more comfortable than I am when I'm with you, Gav. It seems only fitting that I should be at my most comfortable when I finally get to marry the man I've loved for so long, I can't recall a time when I didn't love you."

Gavin released one of her hands to wipe his eyes.

"For a while there," Ella said, "I didn't think you and I were going to happen. I didn't think we'd get our happily ever after. It took a while for you to come around…"

Gavin laughed as he contended with more tears.

"But when you did come around, when you finally saw that my way was the right way, you made me so, so happy. I can't wait to see what's next for us and our little family. I can't wait to add to our family, although maybe not right away," she said with a grimace and a laugh. "I can't wait for everything with you. I, Ella Abbott, take you, Gavin Guthrie, to be my husband. To have and to hold from this day forward, forsaking all others, to love and honor all the days of my life."

Elmer dabbed at his eyes and turned to Gavin. "Gav?"

"Whew," Gavin said. "Not sure how I'm supposed to follow that." He wiped his eyes again and made an effort to pull himself together. "To say I was in a bad place before you, Ella, is putting it rather simply. I was a wreck. An emotional disaster area. The ultimate fixer-upper. But you, my fearless, tireless, relentless love, you only saw the potential, not the mess. You stuck with me through all the hard times and led me through the darkness back into the light that shines all around you." He tucked a strand of her hair behind her ear and caressed her face. "You are, quite simply, my lifeline. You're the reason I get up in the morning, the reason I continue to try when I used to think it wasn't worth the bother. You're the reason for everything. You and our Sarah and the family we're building together have put me back together and given me love and hope and the kind of comfort I didn't know I needed until I had you. Thank you for never giving up on me when anyone else would've quit. I love you so much, Ella. I, Gavin Guthrie, take you, Ella Abbott, to be my wife. To have and to hold from this day forward, forsaking all others, to love and honor all the days of my life."

Everyone in the room was dealing with tears by the time Elmer handed Ella's ring to Gavin.

"I give you this ring as a sign of my love and fidelity," he said as he put it on her finger.

Elmer handed Gavin's ring to Ella.

She slid it onto his finger and looked up at him. "I give you this ring as a sign of my love and fidelity."

"By the power vested in me by the state of Vermont," Elmer said, "I declare you beautiful kids husband and wife. Gavin, you may kiss your wife."

Gavin put his arms around her and stared at her for a long moment before he kissed her and then hugged her carefully, which she appreciated. Every inch of her hurt, but her heart... Her heart had never felt better or been more full.

"I'm pleased to introduce, for the very first time," Elmer said, "Gavin and Ella Guthrie."

Their family cheered for them as Sarah woke up and let out a lusty, angry cry.

It was the most perfect moment of Ella's entire life.

FOR A LONG TIME AFTER EVERYONE HAD GONE HOME OR TO bed, Linc stared at the fire and thought about the remarkable few days they'd had. What was supposed to have been an ordinary holiday-season weekend had turned into anything but, and now the horrible breach with his family had been bridged, and his sons- and daughters-in-law had gone all-out to create a special Christmas for their family. Not to mention the arrival of a new grandchild and a wedding. It'd been a week he'd never forget.

He was truly blessed, and all his blessings began with Molly, who'd turned in hours ago, exhausted as always after the crush of Christmas. He got up, worked around the sleeping dogs to secure the fireplace and went upstairs.

In the hallway, he looked around at the various bedroom doors now standing open and gave thanks for the gift of waking that morning to everyone back in the barn for one memorable night.

He got into bed and was careful not to disturb Molly, but she stirred, nonetheless.

"There you are," she said, sounding sleepy.

"Here I am."

She snuggled up to him, and he wrapped his arms around her. "Was about to send a search party for you."

"Your dad got the whiskey out. It was downhill from there."

"How many times did he use the word 'impertinent'?"

"Only four or five."

"So it was a good night."

"It was a *great* night."

"I'm glad he agreed to stay tonight, too, so he could have a nightcap with you."

"Me, too. I think he wanted to stay close to make sure I'm all right, which I appreciate so much."

"He loves you."

"I know, and I love him right back."

She smothered a yawn. "Did you get a chance to read the Christmas letter from Joseph and Keisha?"

"I did! Jalen is going to be a judge. That's incredible."

"And Jasmine being the national president of an accounting organization."

"I'm glad Keisha finally talked Joseph into retiring at the end of the year."

"Maybe now we can get them back up here for another visit."

"Or meet up with them somewhere."

"That sounds good, too."

He ran his fingers through her hair. "I still can't believe what Cam and the others did while we were gone."

"I know! I was so thrilled. I'd been trying not to think about how I was going to pull off Christmas after being gone the extra day. They made it so I didn't have to worry about a thing. Best Christmas ever."

"It really was. Our amazing kids fell for some equally amazing people."

"They sure did. And just think, it all began at a bus station in Mississippi."

"Best day of my life."

"And mine. Do you still love me more than the Beatles?"

"Always and forever."

"Sing me our song."

In a soft whisper, he gave her the opening notes to the song that had gotten them through the best and worst of times. It had become especially poignant after the split with his family, when Molly and her family had opened their arms to him and welcomed him into their fold. "When I find myself in times of trouble..."

Let it be.

Let it be.

EPILOGUE

wo days after Christmas, Linc slid into their regular booth at the diner, where his father-in-law was already nursing a cup of coffee. "Sorry I'm late."

"Everything all right?"

"My sister called to tell me my father passed away overnight. She said his passing was peaceful, and they were all there with him."

"I'm sorry for your loss, Linc."

"Thank you, but it doesn't really feel like my loss, you know?"

"I understand what you mean, but still... Give yourself a minute to feel it."

Linc nodded and smiled when Megan came over with coffee. "Thanks, honey. How're you doing?"

"I'm still recovering from Christmas."

"Right there with you. Thanks for all you did to help make it happen."

"It was fun and gave us something to do while you were gone."

"You're done after this week, right?" Elmer asked.

"Yes, sir. My temp replacement is due to start later this week so I can show her the ropes."

"No one can replace you," Elmer said.

"Aw, thanks. I'll be around, and I'm sure I'll be here every day with the baby. I won't know what to do with myself."

"Megan," Butch called from the kitchen. "Order up."

"Duty calls."

The door jingled, and Linc's nephew Grayson Coleman came in, smiling when he saw them.

After Grayson hung his coat on a hook by the door, Elmer moved over to make room for his grandson.

"What're you two up to?" Gray asked. "Solving the world's problems as usual?"

"Mostly still recovering from too much Christmas," Elmer said.

"That was a throwdown and a half," Gray said. "Thanks for including us and the rest of the Colemans."

"Of course we included you," Linc said. "And I hear there's more partying in store on New Year's Day at your mother's."

"That's right. All the Colemans will be there, or so I'm told."

"Did you ever hear from Noah the other day?"

"Nope, he was a no-show for Christmas and wasn't answering his phone. I went by his place, and his truck was gone, but I saw it at the inn this morning. Wherever he went, he's back to work today."

"Our international man of mystery," Elmer said.

Megan brought Grayson a mug that she filled after setting it on the table. "Breakfast?"

"Yes, please," Gray said. "I'll have the usual."

"Coming right up."

"How does she remember everyone's 'usual'?" Gray asked.

"It's her special gift."

"So I did hear one thing about Noah that you might find interesting," Gray said.

"What's that?" Elmer asked.

"One of the guys who works for him is a high school classmate of mine. I ran into him at the grocery store two days before Christmas. He told me that Noah and the architect that Mrs. Hendricks hired to redesign the inn have been locking horns big-time. Like full-on screaming matches right in front of everyone."

"Is that right?"

"Yep, and... The architect is a woman named Brianna, and according to my friend, she's, as he said, 'a smoke show.'"

"Translation, please," Elmer said.

"She's hot."

One of Elmer's white eyebrows lifted toward his hairline. "Is that right."

"That's what he said."

"Well, it might be time to stop over at the inn and ask my grandson to give me a tour of the progress."

"I'd be happy to help you with that," Linc said.

"Figured you might, but if this turns into something, it goes in my column."

"Have you two stopped bothering to try to hide the fact that you're minding everyone else's business?" Grayson asked.

Elmer gave him a blank look. "We have no idea what you're talking about."

Grayson lost it laughing. "Whatever you say, Gramps."

Watch for Noah Coleman's story, COME TOGETHER, out on July 13, 2021!

THREE YEARS AFTER HIS MARRIAGE ENDED IN DRAMATIC fashion, Noah Coleman has one goal—to steer clear of romantic entanglements. In fact, he steers clear of most human interaction, studiously avoiding his large, meddling extended family, working until he's exhausted and then repeating the pattern day after day. His strategy has worked well for him for years, keeping him sealed off from anything that can cause him pain or angst. Or it *was* working for him... before his company was hired to rebuild the Admiral Butler Inn after a fire reduced it to rubble, and he was forced to co-exist with the exasperatingly difficult, gorgeous architect the inn's owner, Mrs. Hendricks, hired to oversee the project.

Brianna Esposito is determined to complete the Butler Inn construction under budget and on time—and to make partner in the Boston firm where she's been working fourteen hours a day for five years. Finally, she has a chance to oversee an entire project from start to finish, and to show the firm's leadership that she belongs among their ranks. Nothing is going to stop her from achieving her goal, especially a cranky contractor with the people skills of a rabid cougar. Noah Coleman is the most exasperating human being she's ever had the misfortune to tangle with. She's never had screaming fights with anyone the way she does him, and the fact that he's also the sexiest man she's ever met makes it that much more difficult to hold her ground.

So how is it that when a snowstorm strands her in Butler for Christmas, she ends up spending the holiday with the man she wants to stab one minute and kiss the next? And will he ever tell her why he's so bitter and angry? Brianna suspects the answer to that question could also be the key to his well-protected heart.

Come back to Butler, Vermont to find out if these two adversaries will give in to the sparks that've been flying between them for months or if they'll finally succeed in driving each other crazy.

Preorder *Come Together* now at Marie's store and at online retailers!

Thank you for reading *Let It Be*! I hope you enjoyed the walk back in time to hear more about Linc and Molly's story —and to share Christmas with the Abbotts. I want you to know that I'm fully aware that I took a little liberty with the series timeline by extending a few pregnancies to suit my purposes. I wanted to be there when all the babies arrived, and I thought you would, too. As a result, poor Ella and Megan had or are having the longest pregnancies in the history of the world!

I had the best time writing this book and catching up with all the Abbotts as they enjoy their happily ever afters, and I hope you love it as much as I do. "Let It Be" is my all-time favorite Beatles song, and I'm so glad I was able to give that title—and that song—to Linc and Molly.

A special thank you to Tracey Suppo, who read this book as I was writing it and kept me going with her enthusiasm for all things Abbott. Thank you to my friend and colleague Tia Kelly for the sensitivity read and to my longtime beta readers Anne Woodall and Kara Conrad for their contributions. And thanks to my Vermont beta readers Marchia, Alice, Nancy, Katy, Betty, Jennifer, Doreen, Jessica, Isabel and Deb.

To the home team, Julie Cupp, Lisa Cafferty, Tia Kelly, Jean Mello, Nikki Haley and Ashley Lopez, thank you all for the many things you do to help me every day, and to Melissa Saneholtz and Janet Margot for your help with marketing. To Dan, Emily and Jake, thank you for your support of my career, even when it takes over our house!

This has been a long year for all of us as we navigated life during a pandemic and tried to keep our spirits up in a difficult time. I've been so thankful to be able to lose myself in fictional worlds and to hear from so many of you that my books or characters have brought you comfort. Thank you for that, for your support of my books and your presence in my life. I'm thankful for each and every one of you. I hope you have a wonderful holiday season and that 2021 is a better year for everyone.

Much love,

Marie

ALSO BY MARIE FORCE

Contemporary Romances Available from Marie Force

The Green Mountain Series

Book 1: All You Need Is Love *(Will & Cameron)*

Book 2: I Want to Hold Your Hand *(Nolan & Hannah)*

Book 3: I Saw Her Standing There *(Colton & Lucy)*

Book 4: And I Love Her *(Hunter & Megan)*

Novella: You'll Be Mine *(Will & Cam's Wedding)*

Book 5: It's Only Love *(Gavin & Ella)*

Book 6: Ain't She Sweet *(Tyler & Charlotte)*

The Butler, Vermont Series

(Continuation of Green Mountain)

Book 1: Every Little Thing *(Grayson & Emma)*

Book 2: Can't Buy Me Love *(Mary & Patrick)*

Book 3: Here Comes the Sun *(Wade & Mia)*

Book 4: Till There Was You *(Lucas & Dani)*

Book 5: All My Loving *(Landon & Amanda)*

Book 6: Let It Be *(Lincoln & Molly)*

Book 7: Come Together *(Noah & Brianna)*

The Gansett Island Series

Book 1: Maid for Love *(Mac & Maddie)*

Book 2: Fool for Love *(Joe & Janey)*

Book 3: Ready for Love *(Luke & Sydney)*

Book 4: Falling for Love *(Grant & Stephanie)*

Book 5: Hoping for Love (*Evan & Grace*)

Book 6: Season for Love (*Owen & Laura*)

Book 7: Longing for Love (*Blaine & Tiffany*)

Book 8: Waiting for Love (*Adam & Abby*)

Book 9: Time for Love (*David & Daisy*)

Book 10: Meant for Love (*Jenny & Alex*)

Book 10.5: Chance for Love, *A Gansett Island Novella (Jared & Lizzie)*

Book 11: Gansett After Dark (*Owen & Laura*)

Book 12: Kisses After Dark (*Shane & Katie*)

Book 13: Love After Dark (*Paul & Hope*)

Book 14: Celebration After Dark (*Big Mac & Linda*)

Book 15: Desire After Dark (*Slim & Erin*)

Book 16: Light After Dark (*Mallory & Quinn*)

Book 17: Victoria & Shannon (Episode 1)

Book 18: Kevin & Chelsea (Episode 2)

A Gansett Island Christmas Novella

Book 19: Mine After Dark (*Riley & Nikki*)

Book 20: Yours After Dark (*Finn & Chloe*)

Book 21: Trouble After Dark (*Deacon & Julia*)

Book 22: Rescue After Dark (*Mason & Jordan*)

Book 23: Blackout After Dark (*Full cast*)

The Treading Water Series
Book 1: Treading Water

Book 2: Marking Time

Book 3: Starting Over

Book 4: Coming Home

Book 5: Finding Forever

The Miami Nights Series

Book 1: How Much I Feel *(Carmen & Jason)*
Book 2: How Much I Care *(Maria & Austin)*
Book 3: How Much I Love *(Dee's story)*

Single Titles

Five Years Gone

One Year Home

Sex Machine

Sex God

Georgia on My Mind

True North

The Fall

The Wreck

Love at First Flight

Everyone Loves a Hero

Line of Scrimmage

The Quantum Series

Book 1: Virtuous *(Flynn & Natalie)*
Book 2: Valorous *(Flynn & Natalie)*
Book 3: Victorious *(Flynn & Natalie)*
Book 4: Rapturous *(Addie & Hayden)*
Book 5: Ravenous *(Jasper & Ellie)*
Book 6: Delirious *(Kristian & Aileen)*
Book 7: Outrageous *(Emmett & Leah)*
Book 8: Famous *(Marlowe & Sebastian)*

Romantic Suspense Novels Available from Marie Force

The Fatal Series

One Night With You, *A Fatal Series Prequel Novella*

Book 1: Fatal Affair

Book 2: Fatal Justice

Book 3: Fatal Consequences

Book 3.5: Fatal Destiny, *the Wedding Novella*

Book 4: Fatal Flaw

Book 5: Fatal Deception

Book 6: Fatal Mistake

Book 7: Fatal Jeopardy

Book 8: Fatal Scandal

Book 9: Fatal Frenzy

Book 10: Fatal Identity

Book 11: Fatal Threat

Book 12: Fatal Chaos

Book 13: Fatal Invasion

Book 14: Fatal Reckoning

Book 15: Fatal Accusation

Book 16: Fatal Fraud

First Family Series

Book 1: State of Affairs

Historical Romance Available from Marie Force

The Gilded Series

Book 1: Duchess by Deception

Book 2: Deceived by Desire

ABOUT THE AUTHOR

Marie Force is the *New York Times*
bestselling author of contemporary
romance, romantic suspense and erotic
romance. Her series include Gansett
Island, Fatal, Treading Water, Butler
Vermont, Quantum and Miami Nights.

Her books have sold more than 10 million copies world-
wide, have been translated into more than a dozen languages
and have appeared on the *New York Times* bestseller more
than 30 times. She is also a *USA Today* and *Wall Street Journal*
bestseller, as well as a Speigel bestseller in Germany.

Her goals in life are simple—to finish raising two happy,
healthy, productive young adults, to keep writing books for
as long as she possibly can and to never be on a flight that
makes the news.

Join Marie's mailing list on her website at *marieforce.com*
for news about new books and upcoming appearances in
your area. Follow her on Facebook at *www.Facebook.-
com/MarieForceAuthor* and on Instagram at *www.instagram.-
com/marieforceauthor/*. Contact Marie at
marie@marieforce.com.

Made in the USA
Monee, IL
22 December 2020

55303667R00144